BEDDED AND WEDDED FOR REVENGE

BEDDED AND WEDDED FOR REVENGE

BY

MELANIE MILBURNE

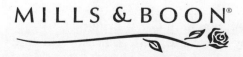
MILLS & BOON®

First published in Great Britain 2006
Large Print edition 2007
Harlequin Mills & Boon Limited,
Eton House, 18-24 Paradise Road,
Richmond, Surrey TW9 1SR

© Melanie Milburne 2006

ISBN-13: 978 0 263 19458 6

Set in Times Roman 16½ on 19 pt.
16-0607-54735

Printed and bound in Great Britain
by Antony Rowe Ltd, Chippenham, Wiltshire

To Ireneanne (Blissie) Aldrich-Briggs.

You have been one of my closest friends for so long, believing in me, loving me, encouraging me and being there for me. I dedicate this book to you in honour of your friendship, which I value so much.

Thank you.

CHAPTER ONE

'BUT you *have* to marry me!' Gemma said in desperation. 'I have less than a week until my birthday. I'll lose everything if you don't!'

The mechanical whir of Michael Carter's wheelchair as it moved even further away made Gemma's blood suddenly chill in her veins.

He was her last hope.

Everything she had been through—everything they had both been through—all the heartache and suffering would have been for nothing if he didn't follow through on their agreement.

'I can't do it,' Michael said, actively avoiding her panicked eyes. 'I thought I could but I can't. It wouldn't be right.'

'Right?' She almost coughed the word out as if it were acid burning her throat. 'What's not right about claiming what is rightfully mine? You agreed on the terms, for goodness' sake!'

'I know, but things are different now.'

Gemma stared at him in rising alarm. 'Do you want more money?' she asked, mentally tallying how much she could afford to siphon off from her late father's estate. She'd have to sell The Landerstalle Hotel but that was the very least of her worries. She didn't want it anyway.

She gave Michael another penetrating look. 'Is that what this is about? You want more money?'

He turned the chair with a deftness she had always privately admired, his grey eyes filled with a shadow of something she hadn't seen there before. 'Listen, Gemma, you know I can never be a proper husband to you…'

'I don't want a proper husband!' she said. 'You of all people know that.'

'I'm sorry…you must think I am deliberately letting you down, but nothing could be further from the truth,' he said.

Tears sprouted in Gemma's cobalt-blue eyes but she fought them back with the determination that had become her trademark ever since the accident that had changed both their lives for ever.

'I can't do this without you, Michael. It's only for six months. *Six lousy months!* Is that so much to ask?'

His eyes moved away from hers again. 'I have other plans… I'm going away. Overseas maybe… I feel I need to put some distance between my past and my future.'

'But what about *my* future?' she asked. 'Without you I have no future! You're the only one who can help me. I need a husband in less than a week otherwise…' She couldn't even say the words out loud; they were just too painful to articulate.

'Look, I'm sorry, but that's just the way it is,' he said, his tone hardening. 'I can't do it. You'll have to find someone else.'

She gave him an incredulous look. 'Look at me, Michael. I'm not exactly model material these days. How on earth am I going to find a husband in less than a week?'

'That's not my problem. Besides, you shouldn't beat yourself up all the time about your looks. You have nothing to be ashamed of.'

No, she thought with a sharp pang of guilt that felt like a rusty saw severing her very soul. *Only the fact that in one senseless act of stupidity I took away both our chances of a normal life.*

She had never really understood Michael's grim acceptance of the consequences of that terrible day, even now almost five and a half years on. Both she and Michael had no memory of the actual accident, which was a small mercy, she supposed. However she did vaguely remember driving to Michael's house after yet another heated argument with her stepmother, but the details of that particular exchange remained locked inside her head.

Michael had never openly blamed Gemma, but just lately she'd sensed a subtle change in him. She saw it now, and a part of her wondered if that was why he was pulling the plug on their agreement as a final act of retribution for what she had done to him.

'I have to go,' he said into the heavily bruised silence. 'I have someone picking me up.' He activated his chair to come a little closer and held out his hand. 'Goodbye, Gemma. I hope things work out for you. I really do. I think it's best if we don't see each other again. We both need to move on from…that day.'

She looked deep into his eyes, but he seemed to be uncomfortable holding her gaze. 'Goodbye, Michael,' she said, forcing her tone into cold, hard indifference when instead she felt as if everything inside her were falling apart piece by piece.

She stood like a frozen statue a few minutes later as a young man arrived to help Michael out to a waiting vehicle, which was fitted with a special wheelchair-lifting device. They drove off soon after with a cough and choke from the spluttering engine of the aged van, which seemed to her to be an added insult considering the amount of money she had offered Michael to be her husband for six months to fulfil the terms of her father's will.

Gemma was still standing in the frame of the open door when a shiny black Lamborghini pulled up in front of her small cottage a short time later. She watched as a tall, vaguely familiar figure unfolded himself from the luxury car and began to move with long strides towards her front door.

She couldn't for the life of her remember where she had met him before. Perhaps he had been a guest at The Landerstalle some time in the past, or maybe he was someone famous. He certainly had an aura of celebrity about him. He moved with an easy long-legged grace, his leanly muscled form indicating he was no stranger to regular hard exercise. He was well over six feet tall and had glossy black hair that was fashionably arranged in one of those casual styles that looked groomed and yet messy at the same time. Even without the luxury car he drove she could tell he was wealthy. His clothes screamed designer and fitted him superbly.

Gemma normally would have quickly closed the door and ignored the bell if it rang, but her intrigue got the better of her.

She hardly *ever* had visitors.

She couldn't remember the last time someone had called on her spontaneously; even Michael had had to be lured to her house by a home-cooked meal, a vintage wine and a recently released DVD.

'Miss Landerstalle?' The man greeted her with a heavily accented voice, which, combined with his dark good looks, indicated his unmistakable Italian heritage.

'Yes,' she said, keeping her hand close to her side in spite of his politely proffered one.

She felt at a distinct disadvantage not being able to recognise him, for she felt sure she should. His commanding presence was almost palpable. Even a little threatening…

'Do you not remember me?' he asked, looking down at her with eyes so brown they reminded her of the colour of espresso coffee.

Gemma felt a strange sensation pass through her at his words. There was something about that deep velvet voice with its clear-cut diction and those darker-than-night eyes that triggered a memory, but she couldn't quite put her finger on it. The accident had wiped some parts of her memory from her brain; she had snatches occasionally of her previous life but most of it she was glad she didn't remember in any detail.

'Um…no…I'm sorry…' she said, uncertainty shadowing her eyes. 'Have we…met before?'

He gave her an unreadable little smile. 'Yes, we have—many times. But it was a very long time ago.'

Gemma stared up at him, suspended in doubt as a crawling fear began to make its way from the base of her spine to the back of her neck on long spidery legs. She moistened her mouth and, taking a shaky breath, said, 'Y-you seem sort of familiar…'

'Allow me to reintroduce myself.' he said, his gaze holding hers like a laser beam. 'My name is Andreas Trigliani. I used to work for your father at The Landerstalle Hotel ten years ago.' He paused for a fraction of second before adding, 'I was one of the bellboys.'

Gemma felt as if someone had suddenly lunged at her mid-section with a thick, solid pole. It truly felt as if a part of her insides had caved in. All her breath was knocked out of her in one fell swoop, leaving her light-headed and weak-kneed. Her memory returned with a rush of shame at how she had treated the young man who had tried so hard to please her all those years ago. Andreas Trigliani's infatuation with the only daughter of the owner of the prestigious Landerstalle Hotel had been an object of amusement to her at the time.

How she had laughed behind his back with her friends—a bellboy in love with her!

A bellboy thinking he had a chance with the sole heiress to a massive fortune!

A twenty-one-year-old Italian boy who could barely string a couple of words of English together!

No, that wasn't entirely fair, Gemma recalled with another sharp twinge of guilt. He had spoken quite good English but she seemed to remember she had ridiculed it all the same. She inwardly cringed at how she had been back then. How could she have been so cruel?

But why was he here now? He didn't look as if he lifted anyone's luggage around now. He looked as if he was used to being waited on, his every whim taken care of with a simple flick of one of his tanned, long-fingered, well-shaped hands.

He had changed so much physically it was no wonder she didn't recognise him at first. He would be thirty-one now—a man in every sense of the word. Ten years ago he had been a shy, eager-to-please young boy, underdeveloped for his age, she had thought at the time, certainly compared to the street-smart and pumped up young men she had frequently associated with. There had been a refreshing innocence about him back then which to her shame she had used to her advantage.

She had treated him appallingly, unforgivably.

'I'm sorry…' She lowered her gaze hoping he wouldn't be able to read the lie for what it was. 'I can't remember… I—I had a serious car accident a few years ago. There are still parts of my memory missing.'

'I am so very sorry,' he said, his tone sounding so genuine it lifted her gaze back to his involuntarily. 'That must indeed be very difficult to deal with.'

Gemma felt his gaze lock down on hers, her heart starting to thump behind her ribcage like a delicate timepiece suddenly way out of control. Her eyes fell away from his again as she answered in a tone that was husky and far too soft, 'Yes… yes…it is…'

There was a long pulsating silence.

Gemma felt the scrutiny of his dark, unfathomable gaze. She could feel the weight of it even as she actively avoided it. It probed her, seemingly laying open her hidden secrets, the shame she had tried to hide from everyone, the shame of her wasted youth, the shame of her past and the shame of her inner wounds that no hand could reach inside and heal.

'I suppose you are wondering why I am here in Sydney again after so long,' he said, the rich, deep timbre of his voice sending a totally unexpected shiver of sensation along the exposed flesh of her arms.

She moistened her tombstone-dry lips again and forced her gaze to meet his dark steady one. 'Are you on another working holiday or business this time around?'

His smile revealed even white teeth, but there was no humour in the movement of his lips. 'I am on a mission, you could say,' he said. 'I am expanding my business to include some Australian luxury resort accommodation. I am interested in the Landerstalle.'

'You've certainly come a long way from being a bellboy,' she observed, covering her uneasiness with a glib tone. 'What did you do? Win the lottery or something?'

His eyes grew momentarily hard. 'No, luck had nothing to do with it,' he said. 'I did it the usual way, with good old-fashioned work. I now oversee several billion dollars of luxury real estate across the globe. I am only sad that my father did not live long enough to enjoy the benefits of my success.' He paused for a moment and added, 'He died soon after I returned from my working holiday in Australia.'

Gemma stared at him, struck into silence by her own grief at the recent loss of her own father. She had never guessed that the young man who had worked at her father's hotel in such a lowly manner would one day own his own empire. He had seemed just like any other cash-strapped backpacker working his way around the globe. As far as she remembered there had been no sign of such lofty ambition way back then.

'I'm very sorry about your father...' she said, knowing how hopelessly inadequate it sounded, but feeling the need to express her sympathy all the same.

'Thank you,' he responded, his tone softening unexpectedly. 'I was very sorry to hear of your loss as well. It must have been very hard on you, being the only child. Over the years I have been very grateful for the comfort of my family to share the ongoing burden of grief.'

Gemma was not used to compassion and felt it strip away her defences, the defences she so desperately needed around herself. She forced her features into a hardened expression and said, 'Yes…well, as you probably remember, my father and I weren't particularly close.'

'He was a good man,' he said. 'A bit ruthless at times but then most men with success in their sight need to be.'

'Yes…' She tried a smile but it made her mouth feel strange. It had been such a long time since she'd used those particular muscles she suspected they had forgotten how to do it.

'How is your stepmother?' he asked.

She gave him a guarded glance before looking away. 'Waiting as we speak with bated breath for my father's estate to drop into her hands,' she said with undisguised bitterness.

There was another silence, shorter this time but no less unnerving to Gemma.

'So your father has left her everything?' Andreas asked.

She dragged her gaze back to his. 'Not exactly, but as it turns out she's going to get the lot after all.'

'Why is that?'

'Because the terms of my father's will state that, unless I am married by my next birthday and stay married for six months, Marcia will inherit the estate in its entirety.'

Andreas looked puzzled. 'Why did he construct his will in such a way?'

'I'm not sure…' She worried her bottom lip with her teeth for a moment before continuing, 'I guess he kind of figured I'd never consider marriage unless he held a carrot too big to resist in front of my nose.'

'The state of marriage does not appeal to you without a suitable inducement?'

She inspected his face for a moment, wondering why he hadn't commented on the thin white line on her forehead that her blonde fringe didn't quite cover, or her ungainly limp, which he surely must have noticed when she had greeted him at the door.

'I am not exactly in tip top shape,' she said with a touch of wry humour that she could immediately tell was completely wasted on him. It was wasted on her as well. There was nothing funny about how her body looked and felt these days.

'You are a very beautiful woman, as indeed you were ten years ago,' he said. 'Any man would be proud to have you as his wife.'

Gemma hunted his dark gaze for any sign of mockery, the mockery she surely deserved after what she had done to him, but surprisingly she could see nothing there but sincerity. 'Thank you.'

'When is your birthday?' he asked.

'In six days' time,' she answered on the tail-end of a ragged sigh, the fluttering sensation of panic in her stomach making her feel physically ill. 'My fiancé left a few minutes before you arrived.'

'Left?'

She gave him a cynical, jaded look. 'Left as in permanently. The wedding is off.'

'I am sorry to hear that.'

She crossed her arms over her chest as if she was cold although the temperature outside was typical of a Sydney sultry summer coming to an unwilling end. 'Not as sorry as me, I can assure you.'

Another silence crept into the space between them.

Andreas moved across the room to stand just in front of her. 'What if you were to find another person to take his place?' he asked.

Gemma had to crane her neck to meet his eyes. She was so used to bending down to Michael's level it had been a very long time since she had met a man's gaze of above average height.

'In less than a week?' She gave him a defeated look and added, 'Things might be very different in whatever part of Italy you come from, but, let me tell you, here in Australia it takes a whole lot longer than six days to find a husband, or at least a legal one.'

'What if I could come up with a solution to your problem within that short space of time?' he said, his eyes steady on hers.

'A solution?' she put in warily, watching that dark, hawklike gaze with an almost fevered concentration, her heart missing another beat.

'You need a husband,' he said as if stating the simple everyday need of replenishing the refrigerator with milk.

'Um…yes…I do…but I hardly think—'

'I am available to fulfil that role for you,' he cut across her protest as if he had known it was coming and had prepared for it. 'It will not be difficult for me to organise the legal details. I have the necessary connections that will see to it without delay. I am willing to step into your fiancé's place.'

Gemma stared at him in a bewildering combination of indescribable fear and a growing sense of relief.

Here was the solution to her problem.

He was offering to marry her. She wouldn't have to lose the estate she needed so desperately… but she couldn't help feeling something about this was all wrong.

'Why?' She almost barked the word at him. 'Why would you want to do that?'

His dark eyes gave nothing away as they meshed with hers. 'You need a husband in a hurry, do you not?'

Gemma wished she could deny it, but the truth lay in a sheath of documents with her late father's lawyer even as the clock on the wall ticked steadily, inexorably towards her birthday.

'Yes…yes, I do, but I—'

'I am willing to step into the role.'

'Why?' The single word burst from her lips again as suspicion began to trickle into her body.

'I need a wife.' He gave a shrug that could have meant anything or everything. 'You need a husband.'

She gave him a narrowed glance. 'As simple as that?'

'I am now thirty-one years old,' he said with an element of pragmatism. 'I am at a time of life when I wish to put down some roots. I am Italian—the desire to have a wife, and family, is in my blood.'

'You don't even know me.'

'Allow me to correct you,' he said with another little enigmatic smile. I know you very well— that is of course unless you have changed dramatically in the last few years.'

It was on the tip of Gemma's tongue to confess that she *had* indeed changed dramatically, but the words stayed locked in her throat. She had covered the truth with a tiny white lie about her memory loss with regard to him and now it would take many more little white lies to keep that one in place. There was so much she didn't remember about the accident and parts of the past, but she had not forgotten Andreas Trigliani and her treatment of him, which confused her as to why he was coming to her rescue now.

He of all people would surely be after revenge. She had ruthlessly bludgeoned his male pride and she could hardly imagine him forgiving her for it unless he, too, had changed dramatically.

He had certainly changed physically over the years. When he had worked at the hotel he had not yet reached his full height, and in young adulthood his limbs, though lean, had not been as heavily muscled and well defined as they were now.

Andreas Trigliani was a stunningly handsome man. He could have anyone he wanted, which begged the question as to why he wanted to tie himself to her.

'I'm not sure what you expect to get out of this arrangement,' she said at last. 'I need a husband—yes, but not a real one, or at least only on paper. I offered Michael Carter, my ex-fiancé, a hefty amount of money but somehow I don't think that you would clutch at it gratefully, not when you have more than enough money of your own.'

He looked at her for a lengthy moment without speaking, his dark gaze still centred on hers.

Gemma felt the silence crawling around her insidiously as if it contained an invisible threat. She could feel it rising up to choke the very breath out of her lungs, her pulse rate starting to hammer in escalating apprehension at the determination she could see in his deep brown eyes.

'I will marry you, Gemma,' he said, speaking her Christian name out loud for the first time in a decade. 'But I have a couple of stipulations and if those stipulations are not agreeable to you then I shall have no choice but to withdraw my offer.'

'S-stipulations?' The word came out slightly strangled as she looked up at him with growing fear in her dark blue eyes.

'Yes,' he said, his eyes glittering with something that struck a chord of unease deep and low in her belly. 'I want a wife but as well as that I want an heir.'

Gemma swallowed deeply but she couldn't seem to find her voice even if she had been able to think of a single thing to say.

Andreas Trigliani paused for a pulsing moment before he continued in the same deep, even tone. 'I will marry you in six days' time on the proviso that you agree to be the mother of my child.'

CHAPTER TWO

GEMMA felt the full blow of Andreas's words as if he'd sent a physical punch along with them, hurting her where she was most tenderly wounded. She held herself together with the steely fortitude that had helped her cope so far, but it was far more tenuous than he could ever have interpreted from the expression she held like a stiff mask on her face.

'That's quite some stipulation,' she finally managed to get out, injecting her tone with a casualness she hadn't believed she could carry off quite so convincingly considering how very shaken she was.

'Perhaps, but it is not the only one,' he continued.

She tried to hold his gaze, but it took a tremendous effort on her part. 'What are the others?' she asked, her mouth feeling as dry as dust.

'When my father died so unexpectedly ten years ago I realised that at some point I would have to fulfil my responsibility to continue the line of the Trigliani family,' he explained. 'I am the only son. It is my duty now to provide an heir. But if our marriage does not work out I insist on having full custody of the child or children of the union. You will have visitation rights of course.'

Gemma had no answer so remained silent. She knew he would immediately see this as an agreement, but she was way beyond caring.

'When this opportunity arose for me to return to Australia I immediately took it. My father would have wanted it this way—wanted me to succeed.'

'You were….very close to your father?' she asked, wondering if he could hear the envy in her voice even though she tried to disguise it.

It was a moment before he answered. Gemma felt as if he was choosing his words with care, that perhaps the subject of his father was still a painful one, even after the passage of ten years. She watched as he sent a hand through the thickness of his hair and noticed that for the first time his eyes showed an emotional depth she hadn't realised was there. It was then that something inside her softened towards him in spite of his outrageous demands.

'My father did not want me to live the sort of life he had lived. He dreamed of one day owning his own hotel. He had spent most of his life working for other people, never feeling financially secure enough to take a holiday for himself. I promised him that I would one day achieve the things he had wanted to achieve. That is why I came to Australia in the first place, to learn the ropes of running a business from the ground up.'

Gemma had been well aware of his success in finding a mentor. Her father had been almost embarrassing in his effusive praise of the young Italian bellboy who had put to shame most of the local lads with his enthusiasm for his work. It had been amusing to Gemma at first, but as time went on she had become increasingly jealous of the attention Andreas had been receiving, attention she had wanted solely for herself. And with a spitefulness that still made her cringe to recall, she had set about getting her father's attention back on her.

Suddenly conscious of the growing silence,

Gemma asked, 'But surely you have numerous Italian women back home who would be much more suited to the task of being your wife?'

'I have had many opportunities, yes, but there are certain advantages to having an Australian wife,' he said.

'A *rich* Australian wife,' she put in.

His eyebrows rose at her. 'Yes, indeed. A very rich Australian wife with the sort of connections I need right now.'

She drew in a cautious breath as she considered his offer. 'So it seems we both can gain from this…er…enterprise?'

'Of course,' he said. 'By marrying me you will inherit The Landerstalle Hotel, which in spite of its somewhat urgent need for refurbishment is still one of Sydney's premier hotels.'

'I want to sell it as soon as I possibly can,' Gemma said.

If her blunt statement surprised him he gave no sign of it on his face. 'It will need a large makeover before you do so, otherwise it will not fetch its true market value,' he pointed out.

'I don't care,' she said. 'I just want it off my hands.'

He gave her a lengthy look, his eyes not once releasing hers. 'But the hotel cannot be sold until the six months is up,' he reminded her.

She stared at him, her growing alarm knocking like a sledgehammer inside her chest. 'You seem very familiar with the terms of my father's will.'

The enigmatic smile was back, those dark, bottomless eyes glittering mysteriously. 'I never do business until I investigate all the angles, Gemma. It is not wise to step into an agreement without covering all bases. Important details could get overlooked.'

She had to lower her eyes from the burning probe of his. 'I have no interest in the hotel. I just need the money from my father's estate to…to settle some bills that have banked up.'

'I will buy the hotel from you when the six months is up for whatever price you care to name,' he said. 'I will also put up the funds for an immediate makeover, which I do not expect you to pay back.'

It was a very generous offer, Gemma thought, but there was only one problem, an insurmountable one that she couldn't possibly inform him of without devastating consequences.

'And in return I will give you what you desire the most—' she disguised a tiny nervous up-and-down movement of her throat '—a child?'

'That is the agreement,' he said.

Gemma felt her stomach tilt in dread. If he were ever to find out how she was deceiving him, what would be the price he would insist she pay? But then hadn't she paid the ultimate price already?

How much more could life ask of her?

No matter how she felt, she had no choice but to block the pricks of her conscience and go with the offer as it stood. But she was short-changing him in a way that was despicable but born out of desperation. She hated herself for what she had to do, but she knew she would hate herself even more if Marcia were to step in and take what her father had worked so hard for and by doing so remove Gemma's last chance to do something good with her life.

Tying herself to a man she had treated so appallingly in the past, a man she'd barely known ten years ago, let alone now, was a small sacrifice to pay, or at least minuscule to what she had paid so far.

Andreas Trigliani seemed a reasonable man, a

very decent man who had clearly forgiven her for her childish and brutally cruel rejection of him all those years ago.

Or had he?

There was something about all this that made the fine hairs on the back of her neck prickle in apprehension.

'I can see I have shocked you with my proposal,' Andreas said into the silence. 'Under less urgent circumstances I would suggest you take a couple of weeks to consider it, but of course that is impossible. I will need your answer now so I can bring about the legal gymnastics that will be required to procure a marriage licence in time for next Friday.'

Gemma swallowed the lump of guilt that had risen in her throat. She *had* to have her father's estate.

She had to!

Even if it meant deceiving a man who could very well destroy her when he eventually found out the truth. But by then, she reasoned, she would have achieved her goal. She needed that money for reasons she couldn't divulge, reasons worth any suffering Andreas insisted she endure.

'I—I will accept,' she said, trying to avoid his unwavering gaze. 'But I…I have a few stipulations of my own.'

He didn't respond, which brought her gaze back to his, as she assumed was his intention. She found it hard to read his expression; it was as if he was keeping himself at a guarded distance. She could hardly blame him. She hadn't been trustworthy in the past; why should he make himself vulnerable again?

She took a breath and prayed her voice would co-operate and come out firm and steady. 'Although we will be married within a week I will need some time to…to get to know you before we…' she could feel her face heating but soldiered on regardless '…sleep together.'

'But of course,' he said. 'I would not be so crass as to suggest we leap straight into a physical relationship without first developing some sort of understanding between us.'

Gemma was sure the immense relief was evident on her face, but she forced herself to speak calmly and evenly even as her belly quivered at the thought of that big, strong, lithe body possessing hers some time in the future. 'Thank you. I appreciate your... patience.'

'You will find in time, Gemma, that I am indeed a very patient man,' he said, his tone sounding to her as if it contained a cryptic element to it.

She searched his face, but again it was as if a curtain had come down over it. It was hard for her to separate her feelings of panic from her sense of responsibility, but she could only hope that what she was agreeing to would not cause too much harm in the end.

The marriage only had to last six months; she wasn't sure why her father had placed that particular caveat on it. It wasn't as if he'd known her real reasons for avoiding marriage.

Although she had argued volubly with him for most of her youth and young adulthood about the restraints put on women by the institution of marriage and the expectation that they would willingly reproduce, she had only done it to annoy him, not out of any strong convictions of her own. It was only when the prospect of having a child was snatched away from her by the cruel hand of destiny that she realised her mistake in tempting fate in such a reckless way.

The one thing she wanted more than anything else in the world was now the one thing she could never have.

And Andreas Trigliani was marrying her to give him a child, a child she could never give him.

What would he do when he found out the truth?

'So,' she said, trying to nudge her guilt away by concentrating on the practicalities, 'what do we have to do to get the licence on time?'

'Leave it to me,' he said. 'I have some legal contacts who will be able to fast-track it for me. We will go ahead with the arrangements you made with your fiancé. Was it to be a big church wedding?'

She shook her head, a wry twist misshaping her mouth. 'It was to be a register office ceremony. I didn't quite fancy limping up the aisle of the local cathedral.'

She was suddenly intensely conscious of his dark gaze as it connected with hers and wished she hadn't revealed the vulnerability of her feelings in such a way.

'I am sure you will be a beautiful bride no matter what sort of ceremony is conducted,' he said with a small smile that touched her in a place she hadn't even known existed.

'Thank you.' She lowered her eyes and added, 'But I hope you weren't expecting a white dress and a veil. I'm not what is known as in your country as…virginal.'

He laughed. 'It would hardly be fair of me to expect you to get to the age of twenty-eight without having experienced pleasure in another man's arms, or indeed in several men's arms.'

Gemma was well aware of her past behaviour and how it had given her a reputation for being wildly promiscuous. She had slept with a small number of boyfriends, but an incident that had occurred on the night of her twenty-first birthday party had left her with one memory she would have given anything to permanently erase.

'I have no plans to draw unnecessary attention to this marriage,' she said, quickly veering her thoughts away from her painful memories. 'I am aware that if the press get wind of this they will be out in their droves, so I want to down play things as much as possible.'

'That's understandable. I, too, do not wish to draw unnecessary attention to myself at this time. I am a relatively new citizen to this country and I wish to make my mark without too much speculation on what I am trying to achieve.'

Gemma frowned at his words. 'You're an Australian citizen?'

'That is correct.'

'So…so you're planning to live here permanently?'

He gave her one of his inscrutable looks. 'Is that not what Australian nationals do?'

'Yes…but you're an Italian with heaps of relatives in your home country. It seems a big move…a drastic move to shift your allegiance to another country.'

'I have many distant relatives in Australia and I look forward to meeting them eventually,' he said. 'I still have business interests in Rome and Milan but I thought it time to expand my empire. Sydney is one of the most cosmopolitan cities in the world. It has a beautiful harbour, a climate many tourists are attracted to as well as a standard of living that is one of the most enviable in the world. I thought it high time I tapped into what it has to offer.'

Gemma was having trouble keeping up. She

screwed up her face trying her best to make sense of all she had heard, but none of it seemed to add up. She had hoped he would be here for only the length of time she needed to gain full access to her father's estate.

On the day of her marriage she would receive a proportion of her father's trust fund, which would be just enough to bring about the goal she had aimed for. But she hadn't counted on Andreas being in Australia indefinitely.

'How exactly did you hear of my…situation?' she asked with another narrow-eyed look cast his way. 'Did you stumble across it by accident or by some other means?'

He met her wary gaze directly. 'I have been in contact with your father on and off over the last couple of years. He gave me valuable business advice on more than one occasion. I greatly admired him and felt grateful for what he did for me when I was young and more than a little wet behind the ears, as I think it is described in English.'

Gemma stared at him in shock. Since when had her father rekindled the relationship she herself had deliberately severed? But then, she reminded herself, she hadn't spoken to her father in close to five years.

'So you owe your success to him?' she ventured.

The enigmatic smile was back. 'In a way— yes. He taught me by example. He treated me with the respect he afforded all his employees from the ground up. His philosophy, as you may or may not recall, was that no matter how lowly a position a staff member occupied it was important to show them your respect at all times. I saw him stop and speak to cleaning staff or financial controllers or managers with exactly the same respect. It was what I most admired in him.'

And what you most despised in his eighteen-year-old daughter, Gemma felt like adding, but remained silent. She recalled her taunting, despicable behaviour with a deep pang of shame. She had been well aware of her father's philosophy, but out of a perverse desire to inflict hurt on him had deliberately not adopted it herself. She had looked down her nose at cleaners and maintenance staff, deeming it beneath herself to mutter even a simple greeting, and subsequently developed a reputation as a cold-hearted, stuck-up little prima donna. As for the rest of the staff, including the various business managers and reception personnel, she had been just as scathing in her dealings with them.

But in spite of how her father had treated Andreas Trigliani in the past it seemed strange that he had appeared now, at the last minute, to offer her help when she needed it most.

'It seems rather coincidental to me that within minutes of my fiancé Michael Carter leaving, you step into the breach.' She sent a suspicious look in his direction.

'It was no coincidence,' he said. 'Your father spoke to me a short time before he died and expressed his concerns over your future. He did not think Michael Carter was the right husband for you.'

'I don't recall ever telling my father I was planning on marrying anyone.'

'Perhaps not, but he assumed of all the candidates most likely to agree it would be Mr Carter.'

'Why?' She sent him a blistering glance. 'Because he was confined to a wheelchair, put there by me?'

Andreas held her accusing glare for a long time before speaking. 'I do not think that was the most pressing issue—no. I believe he felt you were on a pathway to destruction that he wanted to avoid if he possibly could.'

'I don't believe you.' She swung away in anger, turning her back to him.

'No, perhaps not, but the truth is the truth whether you remember it or not,' he said. 'Your father did not trust Michael Carter. He was concerned that in the end he would not have your best interests at heart.'

Gemma turned back to face him, her face a portrait of cynicism. 'And he thought you did?'

'I am committed to bringing about the goals of both your father and myself,' he said. 'I am also committed to bringing you what you have been vainly searching for ever since I met you on the doorstep of The Landerstalle Hotel ten years ago.'

She frowned at his words, her heart doing a funny kick-start in her chest. 'Are you saying you have never forgotten me?'

His wry smile tilted the edges of his mouth, making his dark eyes suddenly glint. 'You are not exactly the forgettable type, Gemma.'

Her forehead furrowed even deeper as the

mortifying memories washed over her; the heat of her cheeks making her feel as if someone had stoked a furnace inside each one.

It was no wonder he hadn't forgotten her. She had been appalling; she had behaved with no scruples and a total lack of grace. She had hurt so many people and it had backfired on her terribly.

Gemma became conscious of him looking at her intently.

'So you do remember a little of our past, Gemma?'

She sent him a brief glance, hoping he couldn't see the guilt in her eyes. 'I told you….I lost parts of my memory in the accident. There is very little I remember of…that time…'

He smiled again and, reaching out, touched her bare arm with one of his long fingers in a soft as air caress that sent a riot of electric sensation the length of her arm and right through the rest of her body. She could even feel the fine hairs on her arms lift up in response to his touch.

'Do not worry yourself, *cara*,' he said in a deep

velvet tone that sent another shiver of feathery sensation up and down her spine. 'We will take each day as it comes. It is not important if you do not remember everything that occurred between us. What is important is the here and now. We have a wedding to organise and limited time in which to do it. Once that is officiated we will then turn our attention to the details of our married life together.'

The details.

Gemma's heart tightened involuntarily at what those details might entail.

She was agreeing to marry a man she had intimated she could not remember when every moment of their acquaintance was stamped indelibly on her brain.

She remembered every word they'd ever exchanged.

She recalled every insult and every mocking laugh she'd shared with her shallow friends.

And she remembered each and every word of that one little lie she had told her father about Andreas, the little lie that had been blown out of all proportion, sending him home to Italy in disgrace.

Her stomach gave another sickening lurch of panic.

God only knew what Andreas would do if he ever found out how she was deceiving him.

CHAPTER THREE

IT WAS no surprise to Gemma that once Andreas Trigliani set his mind to a seemingly impossible task he would in fact pull it off with consummate ease. She had been expecting and mentally preparing herself for a bureaucratic nightmare in acquiring a last minute marriage licence, knowing that it usually took a month, and yet three days later he procured it with a little smile of victory.

She looked down at the document wondering what legal strings he had pulled, but with just three days for her goal to be reached she had no choice but to express her gratitude in a low, barely audible mumble as they prepared to leave for dinner.

The legal document was a chilling reminder to her of the power he could yield if pressed to do so. He had money, lots of money and the sort of connections that gave him an advantage she had no hope of matching.

'I thought tonight would be a good time to go over our domestic living arrangements,' he said once they were seated in the restaurant on the waterfront of one of Sydney's premier eastern suburbs a short time later.

Gemma had been expecting the topic to be raised, but the thought of sharing accommodation with a man she barely knew was terrifying to say the least. She had become used to her own space—craved it, in fact. She hated sharing bathrooms and kitchens, hated anyone seeing her without the concealing make-up that lessened the starkness of her scarred forehead. She hated anyone seeing the stiffness and lack of co-ordination of her leg, which plagued her first thing in the morning until she'd moved around a bit to get the blood flowing in the damaged limb.

'But I like where I live,' she said in a last-minute show of defiance. 'I like the area and the rent is affordable.'

'So you don't actually own the property?'

She gave him an ironic look. 'Do you think I would be marrying a man I don't even remember meeting if I could simply solve all my financial problems by selling my house?'

'No, you are right, of course,' he said. He waited for a moment before adding, 'But the price of a small cottage is not going to sort out the rest of your financial problems, is it?'

Gemma lowered her gaze. 'No.'

'What sort of debt are you carrying at present?'

'The usual stuff…credit-card bills, that sort of thing. But more than that I don't want my step-mother to have what is not rightfully hers.'

'She was married to your father for a number of years,' he pointed out reasonably. 'Surely she is entitled to something?'

Her look was cold and hard. 'Not if I can prevent it.'

Andreas inwardly frowned at her vehement response. Gemma hadn't exactly been the ideal stepdaughter so it hardly seemed fair to lay all the blame on Marcia, who from what he could recall had seemed to be trying her best to conduct a civil if not a little strained relationship with her husband's only child.

He'd met Marcia Landerstalle one or two times in the past and found her to be typical of a lot of second wives. She had been forced by circumstances to take the place of a deceased predecessor who had been elevated to an esteemed position that no living human could ever aspire to. The wicked-stepmother role was more or less a cliché but he still found it hard to accept—considering the track record of Gemma—that Marcia was as bad as her step-daughter intimated.

Of course there would have been rivalry between them. Gemma had had her father to herself from the age of ten and had no doubt found it hard to share him as a young teenager with a woman not much older than herself.

From what he remembered Marcia was dark and exotic, flamboyant and a perfect asset to her husband's business interests, while his daughter had been surly and resentful, prickly and tem-pestuous to say the very least. It had been in many ways a recipe for disaster, but Lionel Landerstalle had been entitled to some sort of life, and while his choice of wife had not pleased his daughter it had certainly brought much pleasure to him. Andreas recalled many conver-sations over the last couple of years where Lionel had praised Marcia's patience and tolerance with regard to Gemma, who had done her best to cause trouble from the get-go. Lionel had come to realise his mistake in listening to his daughter's attention-seeking fabrications and had apologised sincerely for the indignity Andreas had suffered when he had been dismissed without a hearing all those years ago.

'I am afraid staying in your cottage is out of the question,' he said. 'For a start it is too small for two people and as there is no garage I would not like to leave my car out on the street.'

'I don't want to live in the hotel,' she stated intractably.

Andreas watched yet again as a host of emotions flitted over her face. Although he had no intention of living in the hotel he was intrigued as to why she no longer resided there. In the past she had enjoyed having her own private section of her father and stepmother's penthouse, where she had lived life to the full, being waited on hand and foot, her every whim and indulgence attended to by the staff.

'What are your objections?' he asked.

'I don't like the impersonality of living in a hotel,' she said, her mouth coming close to the sort of pout he remembered all too well. 'I've never liked it. The staff members are constantly changing and you never know who is going to bring you your linen from one day to the next. I don't want to live or visit there ever again.'

Andreas frowned at her intransigent response, wondering what had precipitated it. It hadn't surprised him that she wanted to sell the hotel; her father's will and the ends she had gone to to fulfil the terms clearly demonstrated her desire to set herself up financially for a very long time, but what had intrigued him was how soon she wanted to offload it. The prime situation of the building, in the middle of the city, irrespective of its needs for an immediate makeover, did not take away from its inherent value. With a certain amount of money spent it would again be up there with the best that Sydney could offer. Why not wait for the highest bidder?

It also puzzled him as to why she preferred to live in a small inner city cottage. The fortress-like bars at the windows and the row of locks he'd noticed on the front door showed her need for security, which certainly living in a twenty-four-hour permanently staffed hotel would give her. But then, he reasoned, perhaps she preferred her privacy since her accident, preferring to hide her vulnerability.

She was still a very beautiful young woman, but it was impossible not to notice the hint of fragility that hung around her like an aura. Her nervous glances and the almost permanent frown than pulled at her smooth forehead demonstrated that her life was nothing like it had been before. The thin white scar just below her hairline was cleverly concealed with make-up and her partial fringe, but there were shadows in her bluer than blue eyes that had never been there before.

Ten years ago she had made a fool of him in every way possible. He had foolishly fallen in love with her and she had led him on, day after day, until the cruelty of her nature had shown its true colours.

There would be no love this time around, he determined. He would marry her so he would have what he wanted, on his terms. He wanted her in his bed and she had agreed to his demands—for money. He never had any trouble bedding beautiful women and he wasn't in the habit of paying for the privilege. Yet Gemma had agreed to his audacious demands... Didn't that prove she was still the same old self-serving, spoilt little rich girl?

'We do not have to live in the hotel,' he said after another small silence. 'The renovations will have to be done in stages with as little disruption to guests as possible, but, as you say, living there would not be ideal.'

'I'm sorry,' she said with a downcast look. 'I feel as if everyone is looking at me there.'

'I am sure you are being overly sensitive.'

She raised her eyes to send him a caustic little glare. 'How could you possibly know what it's like?' she asked, colour firing in her usually pale cheeks. 'I see the way the staff look at me pityingly. There goes the girl who had it all at her well-shod feet. Feet that no longer can wear the sort of heels I used to sashay around in. I can't bear it. I can't bear their pity. I can't bear anyone's pity.'

Andreas allowed a few minutes for her statement to settle amongst the dust of his resentment towards her. Could this really be the same woman who had looked down at him ten years ago with such haughty disdain? The same woman who had irrevocably marred his life? He wanted her to be the same old Gemma so he could enact his revenge. Otherwise what would be the point of him marrying her? He wanted her to beg him to bed her. He wanted to own her. He wanted to be the one this time to trample her pride in the dust the way she had done to him. He had thought of nothing else for a decade. She said she didn't remember him but...

He *wanted* her to remember.

He wanted her to remember every little detail of her treatment of him that had stained his life for so long. His father's sudden heart attack soon after he'd returned to Italy with the shame of Gemma's filthy accusation still ringing in his ears had made him all the more determined to make her pay. He had waited this long to bring about the justice he craved, but, looking at her small, bowed frame in front of him, he had to concede that perhaps the vicissitudes of life had got in first and taken away his opportunity.

But he would still marry her.

Gemma Landerstalle had turned her imperious little nose up at him ten years ago, but this time she would come to his bed and stay there for as long as he wanted her to.

He would make damn sure of it.

'If you have no objection I will make arrangements for your belongings to be shifted to my house in Balmoral. It is within a short walking distance of the beach,' he said, finally breaking the silence that had been humming like an electric current between them.

Gemma looked up in surprise. 'If you already have a house, then why did you suggest we live at the hotel?'

'I did not suggest we live in the hotel,' he said. 'If you recall I simply brought up the subject of living arrangements and you rather forcefully insisted you were no longer interested in living in your former home.'

'It's a hotel, not a home,' she said with a sour look. 'And for your information it was never a proper home to me.'

'Well, perhaps you will feel more at home at my residence,' he said. 'It has wonderful views over Hunters Bay and Rocky Point.'

'Fine,' she responded unenthusiastically.

He frowned again at her tone. 'Look, Gemma,

I understand this is difficult for you, but, after all, I am the one helping you, so the very least you could do is show some measure of enthusiasm.'

She lifted her dark blue eyes to his. 'I am looking forward to having the money that is rightly mine to do with as I wish. If I am showing a little less enthusiasm than you require at sharing my life with a man I can't even remember, then I'm sorry, but there's nothing I can do to change that. It was never in my plans to marry in the first place, but now I have no choice.'

'What about children?' he asked. 'Had you also permanently ruled out that possibility as so many women your age seem to do these days?'

Gemma shifted her gaze away from the questioning probe of his. 'No…no… I had not personally ruled out having children.'

'You planned to be a single mother?'

Gemma wished she could change the subject, but she couldn't think of a way to do it that wouldn't raise his suspicions. 'What makes you ask that?' she asked instead.

'It is clear to me you were only marrying

Michael Carter to access your inheritance,' he said. 'He is paralysed from the waist down. One would assume he would have been unable to provide you naturally with the children you wanted even if you hadn't planned on officially marrying him.'

'How do you know I wasn't in love with Michael?' she asked, adopting a tone that was so close to what she had sounded like all those years ago it unnerved her even as much as it clearly angered him. She could see the tightening of his jaw and the way his eyes glittered darkly as they held hers.

'The Gemma Landerstalle I remember did not have the space in her heart to love anyone but herself,' he said. 'You might have lost your memory, or at least a part of it, but you cannot have lost your personality along with it. I am sure there is still that heartless young woman residing inside that beautiful body even though you do your best to disguise it.'

'Why would I try and disguise it?' she asked with a flash of ire in her eyes.

His expression hardened in cynicism. 'Because you will do absolutely anything to access your father's estate, won't you, Gemma? Absolutely anything. Even commit yourself to a man you claim you do not remember, even going so far as to agree to have his child.'

She sat in a stony silence, not wanting to reveal her true vulnerability. She reminded herself that it didn't really matter what he thought of her. All she needed from him was marriage. She would force herself to be polite and keep him at a safe distance for as long as she could, but if he was convinced she hadn't changed, then that was his problem, not hers.

'You were even desperate enough to tie yourself to a man who couldn't even be a man in your bed, a man who you were going to use to bring about your mercenary goal,' he added in an embittered tone.

Gemma stared at him in shock, anger finally coming to her rescue. 'How dare you speak of Michael in such a way?' she said as she struggled to her feet, knocking over her water glass in the process. 'He is…is…' She sat back down when she noticed the glances she was getting from the neighbouring tables, her fragile hold on her emotions slipping as the stinging tears sprouted from her eyes and began to slide silently down her cheeks.

The waiter came over and discreetly removed the glass and replaced it with another one, refilling it before laying a white starched serviette on the spillage and moving away once more.

Andreas had not expected to be moved by Gemma's tears. He wanted to get to his feet and pull her into his arms and hold her against him and very nearly did so, except for the fact that she mumbled a quick 'excuse me' and made her way to the powder room before he could even rise to his feet.

He watched her awkward progress and felt his heart contract painfully. He frowned as he took a sip of his wine, quietly savouring the hint of cinnamon and black cherries as he sat back in his seat, wondering if he was in his right mind getting entangled with her again after all these years. Most people would have moved on, but something in him insisted he revisit the past and put things right according to his standards this time around.

It was a matter of pride—yes, but also honour. He had been devastated, his family shattered by her treatment of him and he had sworn he would have his revenge. He had finally been handed his chance, only to find the woman he had stoked his hatred for had seemingly changed, almost beyond recognition.

But what if it was just an act to get what she wanted? The Gemma of the past would have stopped at nothing to get her way. He had personally experienced her ruthless disregard for his feelings. How could he trust the person she said she was now? She had lied before and would no doubt lie again.

For all he knew her tears might have been an act for his benefit to keep him committed to seeing their marriage through. After all, a lot of money was at stake. She had a lot to lose if he didn't hold to the deal.

He wasn't prepared to make himself that vulnerable. Not again.

Not after the last time.

CHAPTER FOUR

GEMMA came back to their table a few minutes later, her make-up perfectly restored, her cool composure indicating her temporary loss of control was now over.

'I am sorry,' Andreas said, assisting her as she sat back down. 'That was unspeakably cruel of me to speak of your ex-fiancé in such a way.'

'It's all right,' she said, not meeting his eyes. 'It's just Michael has a disability, an irreversible disability that is my fault. I have to live with that even though I don't remember a thing about…the accident.' She chewed at her bottom lip as if by doing so it would unlock her mind, but all it did was remove the lip-gloss she'd so recently re-applied.

'Do you recall anything at all about that night?' he asked after a moment.

Gemma shook her head. 'A little bit… I sort

of have flashes occasionally…but not much of it makes sense. I had an argument with my stepmother, but I don't remember what it was about. We've had so many arguments in the past it's hard to recall any of them in any sort of detail.'

'Does Michael remember anything of the accident and what led up to it?'

'Not a lot,' she said. 'He too was in a coma, but for much longer. They weren't even sure he was going to…to survive.'

'Were you and Michael dating at the time?'

Gemma almost laughed out loud and would have done so if she'd been able to remember how to. It had been so long since she'd felt amusement.

'No, Michael wasn't into women, if you know what I mean,' she answered. 'He didn't come out about it until very recently. It wasn't until his father died about a year ago that he felt free enough to share it with others.'

'But you have always known?'

She met his eyes briefly. 'It's a term we Australians use,' she said. 'It's called Gaydar, you know…as in radar.'

His lips twitched with a smile. 'How long have

you known him? I don't recall him being one of your many suitors ten years ago.'

'No…I didn't know him then…'

'How did you meet?'

Gemma hated recalling the night she'd met Michael. It brought back so many distressing memories, and if it hadn't been for how he had helped her the night of her birthday party she would not have nurtured the relationship as she had.

'We met at…at a party,' she answered, keeping her eyes well down. 'He was partnering an acquaintance of mine. We…got to chatting and I felt comfortable with him. Although our backgrounds were quite different we still shared a lot in common. We had both grown up from a young age without a mother. Compared to a lot of other people I knew at the time he seemed…a little more genuine.'

'In what way?'

'I don't know…I guess I felt he wasn't just being my friend because of my wealthy background. It's hard, you know…' she lifted her eyes back to his momentarily, trying not to reveal her discomfiture as she continued

'...working out who likes you for who you are or what you can give them.'

'So what happened to the host of adoring men that followed you around like lap dogs all those years ago?' he asked.

Gemma lowered her gaze to the food that had been put in front of her and wondered if she could summon up either the energy or appetite to do it justice. 'You know what they say about fair-weather friends,' she said as she made a token effort by picking up her cutlery. 'They're there for the good times but not for the bad.'

'Yes, you are indeed right,' Andreas agreed. 'Once people know you have money they treat you very differently.'

Gemma wondered if he was obliquely refer-ring to her. She had rejected him ten years ago and yet here she was promising to be his wife.

She gave him a tentative glance. 'You inti-mated earlier that my personality cannot have changed...you said I was heartless or words to the effect.'

'I should not have spoken to you like that,' he said, a little frown of remorse bringing his dark brows together. 'It is in the past, the past you cannot remember. It is hardly fair to bring it up. It has nothing to do with the future—our future.'

Gemma looked at him for a moment. She knew they could have no future, certainly not with the past lying between them as it did. And once he found out the truth about her he would no doubt find some way to make her pay for her mendacity.

She stared down at her water glass with its beads of condensation trickling like crystal tears down the sides.

'Have you worked since the accident?' he asked into the silence.

'Sort of…' she answered, glancing up at him again. 'I work at a women's refuge centre but I'm not on the payroll. It's mostly staffed by volunteers.'

She expected him to show some element of surprise on his face, but he simply took a sip of his wine before commenting, 'That must be very demanding but no doubt rewarding work.'

Her eyes fell away from his again. 'It is demanding at times but I can't live for ever without an income. I intend to give it up as soon as I get my father's estate.'

Gemma was conscious of his studied gaze as it rested on her. She was aware of him in a way she had not been of any man. She was uneasy with him as indeed she was uneasy with most men other than Michael, who had posed no threat. Something about Andreas Trigliani made her blood race in her veins and her heart begin to thump unevenly, and it had very little to do with fear at what he could do to her but more to do with what she could be tempted to feel for him if she let her guard down around him. Although he had changed physically, she could still see the gentle, caring nature of the Andreas of ten years ago even though he appeared to be making an effort to conceal it from her. She felt it in his touch, the warmth of his fingers, unlike anything she'd experienced before. It made her flesh ache to feel more of him, to run her hands over him, to explore his hard contours, to trace his sensual mouth with her fingertips to see if it would soften at her touch…

'Why did you choose to work at all when you are an heiress to a fortune?' he asked, instantly jerking her away from her thoughts.

'I wasn't sure I was going to be an heiress,' she

said. 'My stepmother was doing her best to ensure I was written out of my father's will.'

'But she did not succeed.'

'No.'

'So in spite of how you felt about him, your father loved you after all,' he said.

Tears pricked again at the backs of her eyes, but this time she refused to allow them to flow freely. She stared at the blood-red rose on the table and forced her tone into one of hard detachment. 'He had a strange way of showing it, the terms of his will being a case in point.'

'Yes, it is indeed an unusual arrangement,' he commented. 'But then he was an astute businessman who liked to cover all bases.'

'Yes,' she agreed with a cynical twist to her mouth. 'His little caveat that the marriage must last at least six months before the entire estate is finalised clearly demonstrates his lack of trust towards me.'

'You will still be a considerably wealthy woman on the day of our marriage,' he pointed out.

'Yes.'

'So what will you spend it on?' Andreas asked,

his gaze running over her simple black dress and lack of jewellery.

'I have some investment plans,' she said. 'I want to set myself up so I don't have to think about a career.'

'Tell me about your reasons for working at the refuge centre.'

She gave him a quick glance from beneath her lashes as she reached for her water glass. 'I didn't do that well at school. I didn't qualify for medicine as my father had hoped or even for the most basic university degree.' She ran her fingertip around the rim of her glass absently as she continued. 'At first I started working there to annoy my father. He suggested I work at the hotel, you know, in management or something, but I refused. I knew he would be disappointed that his only child had aimed so low, but once I started working at the women's shelter I really began to enjoy it.'

'What did you enjoy about it?'

'I enjoyed seeing women who had suffered turn their lives around...the children too, especially the little ones who were often so bewildered by what had gone on in their lives.'

'I can see you will be a wonderful mother when the time is right,' he said with yet another of his unreadable little smiles.

Gemma had to look away. She could imagine what an adoring father he would be. She knew most Italians valued family very highly. He was clearly no different. Why else was he tying himself to her, an heiress he assumed could give him what he wanted? Not the broken woman she really was.

'I have also enjoyed keeping in contact with one or two women who've managed to rebuild their lives,' she said, more in an attempt to shift her thoughts from a subject she found unbearably painful. 'Not many keep in touch, but one in particular has become a close friend.'

'Tell me about her.'

She knew it was probably asking for trouble to drift into such dangerous waters, but something about his quiet graciousness had got beneath her normally rigid guard. She didn't want to reveal her real reasons for claiming her father's inheritance, but neither did she want Andreas to think she was totally without feeling as indeed she had been towards him ten years ago.

'It's not easy for women to leave a partner who has turned violent,' she said. 'People just assume the woman should up and go, but it's so complicated when young children or even pets are involved. It often takes many attempts before the final severance of the relationship occurs. Also, the involvement of police and protective services put a lot of women off. They often feel they won't be believed or will be criticised for going back time and time again. It's not as simple as everyone thinks.'

Andreas watched the flicker of emotions pass over her still-beautiful face and his heart tightened in spite of all she had done to him in the past. He had hardened his heart for so long, intent on revenge, and yet meeting her again after all this time had taught him that people were not always as they seemed.

She had apparently developed a social conscience, which was perhaps not all that surprising considering what life had dished up to her.

She carried the guilt of maiming a man for life.

Michael Carter was without the mobility he had taken for granted a few short years ago and

Gemma Landerstalle was responsible for it. Although they had both been thrown from the car, the accident investigation report had declared her the driver. She had been charged with negligent driving and even though she had faced a short prison sentence her father had somehow influenced the judge to wholly suspend it and offer her bail instead. But though she claimed she had amnesia it was clear she carried the guilt of her past in some small measure, it was written on her face, she carried it on her body, reminding him of a bruised, fragile orchid in the crush of a hand too insensitive to her delicate needs.

'Do you remember much of your mother?' he asked.

She gave him a rare smile. It was small, hardly moving her mouth at all, but it was still a smile and he couldn't help feeling as if he would like to see it more often.

'Yes…she was beautiful and smelt like perfume all the time,' she said. 'She had blonde hair like me—mine is a bit darker and straighter, but she always looked so elegant.'

'What happened?'

Gemma hated this part. The explanations that everyone wanted and she was so loath to give. Her mother's short, beautiful life reduced to a random illness that could have been prevented if help had been sought in time.

'She died of a ruptured appendix.'

His eyebrows rose. 'In this day and age?'

'It *was* eighteen years ago,' she said, meeting his eyes briefly. 'Septicaemia set in and it was too late by the time my father noticed how desperate things had become. Her organs began to shut down and there was nothing anyone could do.'

'So that is why you have always had such ill feeling towards your father?' he guessed. 'You held him personally responsible for your mother's untimely death?'

'No...it was just one of those things,' she lied, knowing that a thin thread of red-hot anger had woven its way through her life for what she had missed out on because her father had been too busy concentrating on building his own particular empire rather than considering his wife's needs. Her mother had paid the price for his neglect, and Gemma was still in some measure, even now, paying for it too.

'It must have been very hard for you growing up without your mother during your adolescence,' he said. 'Was your stepmother able to bridge the gap at all?'

'My stepmother relished the role of being a surrogate parent,' Gemma said with an unhappy expression. 'She took on the responsibility with an avid enthusiasm that would have impressed anyone.'

'Except you,' he put in, yet again demonstrating his inbuilt percipience.

She couldn't hold his penetrating dark gaze and instead concentrated on taking a tiny sip of her water.

'You haven't touched your wine,' he observed after a small pause.

Gemma looked at the crisp white wine in the glass before her and felt her stomach lurch in revolt. 'I have no real taste for alcohol,' she said with complete sincerity.

'I seem to recall you were quite keen on it in the past.'

Her eyes shifted away from his. 'Yes…well, that may well have been the case, but I have no memory of it,' she lied again.

God, how she had behaved back then, she thought with a savage twinge of mortification. She had been totally out of control, downing whatever liquor was available in an effort to numb the inner pain of her life. It had started with the fruity vodka drinks cleverly marketed at the young, and then she had progressed to the harder stuff. She had downed shot after shot, never thinking it would lead to the destruction of her life in the way it finally had.

'Tell me about your family,' she said to shift the focus away from her guilt.

His face relaxed in a smile that brought out the warmth of his chocolate-brown eyes. 'I have two younger sisters, Gianna and Lucia. They are both married and expecting babies in a few weeks' time. My mother is a wonderful woman who even after all this time is doing her best to cope with her grief. She misses my father dreadfully, more so now as the grandchildren she and he longed for are about to arrive. I would like her to meet you some time soon to take her mind off her loneliness.'

'That sounds like a good idea.' She moistened her mouth. 'But what will you tell her about…us? I mean, won't she be terribly shocked when you tell her you are marrying me at such short notice?'

'My mother is a hopeless romantic,' he said. 'I have already told her of meeting you all those years ago. She will believe me when I tell her that we have found each other again.'

'So…so you'll pretend you're really in love with me?'

'But of course. How else would I explain such a hasty marriage?'

Gemma frowned as she thought about meeting his mother some time in the future. 'But when she meets me… she's surely going to suspect something's not quite right,' she said.

'How so?'

She met his eyes again. 'We don't love each other, for a start, and then there's the issue of when I will feel ready to… to…sleep with you.'

He gave her a lengthy look. 'We will start our marriage in the same bedroom, Gemma, in the same bed. I absolutely insist on it.'

Gemma stiffened in her seat. 'But I don't want to—'

'I told you yesterday that I will not force

myself on you. That would indeed be despicable. We will not consummate our relationship until you are ready to make our marriage a real one. You can trust me on that, although I do not really see what your problem is. You are an experienced woman of the world. It will not be long before the physical attraction that I have always felt for you triggers a similar reaction in you.'

Gemma hoped he couldn't see any trace of the apprehension that she could feel in every pore of her body as she met his gaze. 'You make it sound so…so clinical…as if desire can be turned on and off like some sort of switch.'

'Sometimes it is indeed just like that,' he said with another little cryptic smile.

She looked away in case he saw the guilt reflected in her eyes, for she knew it must surely be there. She recalled all too well how she had flirted with him outrageously, as indeed she had with other young men. She had gone out with him several times, later laughing behind his back with her friends at how he had held doors open for her and pulled out chairs for her to sit on, gazing at her with open adoration at each of the expensive restaurants and nightclubs she'd insisted he take her. He had been nothing but a gentleman the whole time, which—in spite of what she'd told her friends—had secretly impressed her. He had been so unlike the other young men she'd normally associated with. They would have pawed at her with groping hands, but instead Andreas had seemed to respect her for who she was as a person, seeing past the overly indulged young woman to the inner core of her deepest insecurities.

It had threatened her in the end, the way he'd looked at her with that intelligent dark brown gaze, as if he could see the persistent little demons that were gnawing insidiously at her soul while no one else was looking...

'Why do you hate yourself so much, Gemma?' he asked on her return from the powder room where she had rapidly and rather crudely dispensed with the expensive meal he had worked so hard to pay for.

She tossed her head and affected a hard little laugh, all the time trying to ignore the flicker of concern she saw in his eyes. 'I don't hate myself, Andreas. I love myself. Look at me. I'm rich, I'm slim and attractive—what more could a girl want?'

He looked at her with such pity she silently summoned up the anger that had been her armour ever since the day she had watched her mother take her last breath. She wanted no one's pity, least of all that of an Italian bellboy who fancied himself in love with her.

She smiled at him seductively across the table, tantalising him with the promise of her body, trailing her fingers over him in a series of seductive little touches, teasing him with her attentions. 'You want me, don't you, Andreas?' she asked in a breathy whisper. 'You really, *really* want me.'

His eyes darkened and his voice came out rough and deep. 'You know I do.'

She smiled an inward smile of victory. *See, Marcia?* She felt like saying out loud. *Men do find me irresistible in spite of what you think.*

'Well, I want you too, Andreas,' she purred at him. 'I want you to kiss me and touch me and make me feel like a woman.'

Gemma took his hand and led him from the restaurant and back to the hotel to her room, closing the door and leaning back against it, her eyes glittering with purpose. 'Why don't you come and get me, Andreas?' she said with a seductive tilt of one hip. 'Show me what a man you are.'

He stood before her, his expression sober. 'Why are you so frightened of being yourself?' he asked. 'You are not the unprincipled little flirt you make yourself out to be. You are hurting, Gemma, and I will not add to that hurt like the countless others you surround yourself with. I will wait until you come to me as an equal and not before.'

She gave him a scathing look and spluttered, 'An equal? You and me? *Are you joking?*'

'I am a human being the very same as you,' he responded coolly.

She curled her lip at him. 'You're a peasant boy, that's what you are.' She laughed, a cruelly taunting laugh. 'I suppose you think I would have gone through with it? What a joke! I was leading you on. I was never going to sleep with you. *As if!* You haven't got a dollar to your name. You are the very last man on earth I would consider sleeping with. Do you really think I would lower myself in such a way? You wouldn't know the first thing about pleasuring a woman. You're not even a full-blooded man. You haven't even once tried to kiss me.'

'That can easily be remedied,' he said, stepping towards her, his hands settling on her arms like a steel vice.

She reared backwards, a scream coming to her throat.

'What's going on?' The door burst open and Gemma turned to see her father standing there.

It was one of those split moment decisions, a decision she might never have made in another time, another place or another context.

But this time she did.

She ran to her father, throwing herself into his arms, sobbing out just the beginning of one little white lie…

'He was trying to…to…to…'

Her father's protective hug stalled her speech momentarily. When had been the last time her father had held her this close? His arms felt almost awkward around her, as if he didn't quite know how to hold or comfort her. How had it come to this? It seemed everyone was between her and her father…even now Andreas.

She buried her head into her father's solid

warmth and, desperate to prolong his embrace, sobbed out the rest of her despicable lie…

Gemma couldn't believe how ironic it was that Andreas was now a fully grown man, an attractive and sexually compelling man who gave every impression of being very experienced in the art of pleasuring a woman. She had ridiculed him out of fear, never once stopping to think how those words would come back to haunt her. Andreas had a brooding sexuality about him now as if he was simply biding his time, quietly confident he would succeed in his mission to bed her for his pleasure and revenge. It was impossible not to imagine what his body would look like now in the throes of passion, the sculptured muscles of his back and thighs and his maleness between them bringing immeasurable rapture to his lover.

But she could never be that lover.

Not unless she risked the only positive thing she had found in all of the tragedy and mistakes of her life so far.

Her heart…

CHAPTER FIVE

'I WILL send a removal company for your things on Friday morning,' Andreas said, instantly jarring Gemma out of her painful recollections. 'We will be married later that afternoon at three p.m. As soon as it can be arranged I would like us to travel to Italy. I had thought of going to one of the Queensland Whitsunday islands for a short break. I had hoped to visit them when I was here before but was unable to at the last minute. However, my mother and sisters are very keen to meet you so that is my first priority for now.'

Gemma had been too ashamed to ask her father what had happened to the bellboy after he had been dismissed. It had been bad enough witnessing the scene she had brought about in her room. Andreas had stood proudly and silently before her father, never once protesting his innocence. His gaze had only moved the once towards Gemma's, briefly connecting with hers before she'd turned away, but, brief as the connection had been, there had been no mistaking the promise of revenge glittering there.

'Why was your working holiday cut short?' she asked, hoping he couldn't see through the charade of her seemingly innocent enquiry.

He didn't answer immediately and again she felt the compulsion to lift her gaze to his, which she was fast learning was a clever strategy of his to get her to look at him when she most didn't want to.

'I was fired from your father's employ,' he said, his eyes intent on hers.

She unconsciously moistened her dry lips. 'Wh-what for?'

'I was accused of something I did not do.'

She swallowed. 'I'm sure if you'd explained my father would have listened.'

He gave her a grim smile. 'Perhaps he would if I had thought it worthwhile defending myself, but at the time I did not.'

'Why didn't you think it worthwhile?'

His dark eyes held hers like a powerful

magnet. 'Pride is a powerful emotion, is it not, Gemma? I had too much of it and it backfired on me in a way I had never imagined it would.'

Gemma felt her heart tighten in her chest. 'Wh-what happened?'

'My father was relying on the money I was earning to clear some pressing debts. He had injured his back and was unable to work. I had been sending back as much money as I could while I was here, but I had planned on staying for a year at least. When I arrived home questions were asked. I had no choice but to tell him what had occurred.' He paused for what seemed an eternity before adding, 'He died of a massive heart attack the following week. I've always imagined it was from the stress of my ignominious return without the money he needed to salvage the family's financial situation.'

Gemma knew the shock was evident on her face, but there was nothing she could do to disguise it. 'Why didn't you try for another job at another hotel?' she asked.

'Your father made it clear that my name would be black-listed throughout the industry. I had no reason to believe he would not carry out his threat if I sought work elsewhere. I decided it was better to return home before I was tempted to seek the revenge I most desperately wanted.'

Gemma's stomach began to clench in fear. 'R-revenge?'

His eyes were like black diamonds. 'Justice is perhaps a preferable word. I wanted to clear my name, but in the end your father was the one who decided I had been telling the truth. A couple of years ago he called me out of the blue and apologised for his treatment of me. It was generous of him under the circumstances.'

'Why did he change his mind?'

'He no longer believed the other person's account of what had happened,' he answered after another momentary pause. 'Apparently it hadn't been the first time they had lied to him.'

'So…where is your family home in Italy?' she asked in a desperate attempt to redirect the conversation.

'I spent most of my childhood living on the outskirts of Rome, but I now have a holiday property on the Amalfi Coast,' he answered. 'Have you ever been to Italy?'

'A long time ago,' she said, recalling with considerable shame the way she had acted on that one European trip her father had meticulously planned in an effort to get her to get along with her stepmother a couple of years after his remarriage when Gemma was fourteen. 'I remember the Trevi Fountain and the Colosseum and Vatican City. And I remember it was hot and there was a lot of traffic and no one seemed to be obeying the road rules.'

His mouth tilted wryly. 'Yes, that is something that has still not changed. But then Sydney, too, is not unlike that at times.'

'Yes.'

There was another three-beat silence.

'Do you drive these days?' he asked.

She shook her head. 'No. It's probably cowardly of me, but after what I...what happened I can't quite bring myself to take the risk. Besides, I couldn't have afforded to keep a car on the road with petrol prices rising all the time and insurance and so on.'

'Surely your father would have helped you?'

Gemma met his eyes, bitterness reflected in their blue depths. 'In any of your conversations with my father before he died, did he not tell you of my decision to cut all ties with him a few months after my accident?'

'We did not speak often, no more than once or twice a year at the most. When I asked after you all he said was you were being your usual difficult self, not wanting to speak to him or visit him.'

'I had a furious row with him,' she said, looking away. 'It was about my stepmother as usual. I delivered an ultimatum, which backfired. He chose my stepmother's version of events over mine. He seemed to think that just because some parts of my memory were missing I was filling in the empty spaces with nonsense.'

'What is it you do not like about your stepmother?' he asked.

Gemma brought her gaze back up to his, suddenly so close to telling him it surprised her back into silence.

He wouldn't believe her any more than her father had. He, too, would reject what she had to say as a fabrication born out of her selfish, petulant nature.

No one would believe the truth. Sometimes she even doubted it herself, especially since the accident, wondering if her mind had conjured up images just to confuse her.

'Gemma?' he prompted.

'It doesn't matter,' she said, pushing away her barely touched meal. 'My father is dead and because of my pride we were unable to say the things that should have been said to clear the air between us. Now it is too late.'

'He must have been just as proud for he could just as easily have approached you first,' he pointed out.

'Yes...he was proud,' she said, her forehead creasing in a resentful frown. 'I guess that was part of the problem. He didn't like failure. He hated it. He saw me as his biggest failure.'

'I am sure you are misjudging him,' Andreas said.

'Am I?' she asked with a glittering look cast his way. 'Look at me, Andreas. I am hardly what one would call a successful person, am I?'

'You are being very hard on yourself,' he said. 'There can hardly be a person alive who has not made some bad choices and lived to regret them.'

'I wish it had been me instead of Michael,' she

said in a tight little voice as she stared back down at her plate. 'You have no idea how much I wish I could turn back the clock and rewrite the past.'

'It is perhaps a mercy then that you do not recall a great deal of it.'

His wry tone brought her head up, but his expression gave nothing away. 'Yes….' she said with a tiny, almost inaudible sigh. 'Yes…it is…'

The waiter cleared their plates and after Gemma declined dessert or coffee Andreas suggested they leave. He led the way out to his car, helping her get into the low-slung vehicle and stretching the seat belt for her to clip into place. His hand accidentally brushed against her breast and she jerked back as if he had burnt her.

Her reaction surprised him. She had not been so adverse to a man touching her in the past. He had seen the way she had draped herself over her latest beau with no regard for propriety. Her clothes back then had been revealing and provocative, as had been her flirtatious manner, which at the time he had found totally captivating in the blind innocence of his calf love for her.

It was hard to believe it was the same woman

sitting there with what looked like fear tightening every muscle of her body.

Fear or revulsion, he mused as he closed her door and came around to slip in behind the wheel.

He frowned as he mulled over the possibility.

Ten years ago she had rejected him in the most humiliating way possible, leading him on until he had been almost feverish with anticipation, only to slap him down as if he were an overgrown puppy that had got out of hand. He had never forgotten the total devastation of his pride, how hurt he had been. The hurt had gradually turned to anger, a simmering anger that had never quite gone away.

It was still with him now.

He could feel it beating in his blood every time he heard or saw a glimpse of who she had been back then. Sure, people could change over time, but certainly not that much.

He *had* to remember that.

She was not to be trusted. Her father had warned him only a few weeks before he'd died. Gemma had a habit of using people and situations to get what she wanted. She had done it all her life.

She might pretend to be repulsed by his touch now, but he was confident he would have her begging for him within weeks. He thought about possessing her, filling her, taking her to the highest pinnacle of pleasure, the pleasure she had told him he wasn't capable of delivering.

He suppressed a little smile as he drove in the direction of her cottage.

Maybe it wouldn't take him weeks to get her into his bed.

Maybe just days…

Gemma sat silently in her seat, trying to get her heartbeat to return to normal. The feel of Andreas's hand brushing so gently against her had shocked her, but not for the reasons she had expected.

For years she had avoided any man's touch, even changing to a female doctor and dentist for her check-ups in order to avoid triggering the memories of the day her life had been shattered by a man who had stripped her of her dignity by taking her by force while she had been too drunk to do anything to stop him.

But Andreas's touch was nothing like that.

Instead it had stirred deep longings she had thought she no longer possessed in any form.

Even over dinner she had looked at his hands several times, wondering how they would feel against her. He had beautiful hands, long-fingered and tanned, with masculine hairs running down from his arms into light sprinkles on the top of each of his fingers. She wondered what it would feel like to have those masculine hairs lying against the smoothness of her skin. She even wondered what it would feel like to have the dark shadow of his jaw lying against her breasts, the rasp of his skin a heady reminder of his maleness against her femaleness.

She flinched away from her wayward thoughts, but they returned as soon as he brought the car to a standstill in front of her cottage. She glanced at his hand closest her as it pulled on the hand-brake with a strength that showed the muscular definition of his forearm where his shirt sleeve was rolled up against the late summer heat.

She tore her eyes away and stared down at her hands instead, wondering if he'd noticed the changes there. Gone were the talon-like nails, painted in bright look-at-me colours. In their place were ten bitten-to-the-quick excuses for fingernails, the cuticles red and uneven in places where her habit of picking at them had spun out of control in response to the recent stress she had been under.

She tucked them out of sight as he came around to open her door, wishing she could exit the car in the manner she had been capable of in the past with the lithe agility and grace she had completely taken for granted. Instead she was reduced to having to take several preparatory breaths to avoid the flash of pain any sudden movement sent through her damaged leg.

Andreas offered her a hand and this time she took it, curling her fingers around the warmth of his as he helped her out. She tried to disguise her wince of pain, but he must have seen it for he took her by both arms in a gentle but secure hold to steady her. 'Are you all right?' he asked, his expression full of concern. 'You look very pale.'

'I'm fine.' She tried to smile but her mouth wouldn't quite co-operate. 'It's just my leg is a bit stiff after sitting. It will soon loosen up.'

He escorted her to the door, with a hand at her elbow, shortening his much longer strides as she limped alongside him. 'Is the damage to your leg permanent?' he asked.

'It was broken in several places and is held together by a series of nuts and bolts,' she answered as she searched for her key in her purse.

'Is there nothing that can be done to improve it?' he asked, stretching out his hand to take her key.

'It's all right,' she said, referring to the key in her hand. 'I have to dismantle the security system.'

Andreas waited as she punched her code into the key pad and once the door was opened followed her in, closing it behind him.

'No, there's not much that can be done,' she returned to his question about her leg. 'The doctors assured me that over time it will stop hurting so much, but I can't help feeling they were fobbing me off.'

'Do you need something for the pain?' he asked.

She shook her head. 'No…really, I'm fine. I'll do some stretches once you've gone and I'll be as good as new…well, not quite,' she added with a rueful grimace. 'But, unlike some, at least I can still walk.'

She turned away to place her purse on a small table where the telephone was situated. Andreas saw her glance down at the answering machine beside it, but there was no flashing light to indicate anyone had called.

He couldn't help feeling she lived a lonely, isolated life locked away in her little cottage prison.

'Would you like a coffee?' she asked, he assumed out of general politeness rather than any desire to prolong his stay.

'Coffee would be nice,' he said. 'But why not let me make it while you put your leg up for a while?'

Her eyes flashed with the ferocious pride he had always associated with her. 'Please do not pity me,' she bit out. 'I can make a cup of coffee without falling over.'

'I was not suggesting you couldn't. But, as I said a few minutes ago, you look pale. I was only trying to be helpful.'

'I do not need your help.'

'Ah, but you do, Gemma,' he reminded her as he closed the distance between them with a couple of strides. 'You need me more than anything. Without me you will lose everything.'

Gemma couldn't drag her eyes away from the

smouldering depths of his. She could smell the lemon-scented aftershave he wore until her senses began to reel with its intoxicating allure. She could even feel the warmth of his body as it stood so close to hers, making her feel unsteady on her feet, which for once had nothing whatsoever to do with her injured leg.

She held her breath as he lifted a hand to her face, brushing the back of his hair-flecked hand across her cheek in a touch so gentle she felt each and every fine hair on the back of her neck lift in response.

'It would be in your interests, *cara*, do you not think, to humour me until you get what you want?' he asked in a sexy low drawl that sent a reactive shiver along the bare skin of her arms.

She moistened her lips with her tongue, trying her best not to sound breathless. 'Wh-what are you saying?'

He smiled a lazy smile as he tipped up her chin, gazing deeply into her eyes. 'You are a bewitching combination of two women, are you not? The brash, selfish and proud young woman of ten years ago, and the new one, the fragile, sensitive one that I find totally irresistible.'

Gemma had not thought of herself as irresistible in a very long time and tried not to let his compliment get to her, but it was impossible not to respond in some way to the words that held such promise of healing within them.

She wanted to feel beautiful again, beautiful not just in body but in personality and soul as well. Andreas might think she was a combination of two people, but the truth was she was nothing like the young girl she had been in the past. She could never go back to being that sort of person. Not after what had happened. The lessons of life had been hard to learn, but she had learned them well and had no intention of making the same mistakes again.

'I was just a teenager then,' she said in a scratchy whisper. 'I was only eighteen when we met.'

He gave her a suddenly probing look, his fingers on her chin tightening a fraction. 'I thought you could not remember anything about that time?'

Gemma's heart clanged against her ribcage with such force she thought it was going to land at her feet. 'Um...I—I don't...but you said it was ten years ago and I...I did the numbers. I was eighteen...still a teenager...sort of...'

He seemed to accept her answer as the truth, for his hold relaxed. His thumb roved a pathway across her bottom lip as he continued to hold her gaze for a moment before he lowered his eyes to her mouth.

Gemma watched as his head came closer and closer, but she did nothing to step out of the reach of his mouth as it finally settled on hers.

His kiss was soft, softer than she'd been expecting and certainly softer than anything she'd experienced before. But although the movement of his lips upon hers was gentle she could still feel the electric current of sensations just under the surface of both of their mouths, making hers tingle and ache for more pressure and the total possession of his tongue.

But, as if he didn't want to deepen the kiss any further, he stepped back, looking down at her with an expression on his darkly handsome features she had no hope of decoding.

'I think I will not have that coffee after all,' he said after a tiny pause. 'It will no doubt keep me awake all night.'

Gemma stood uncertainly before him, silence her only refuge. She watched as he turned for the door, deftly releasing the four locks before leaving without another glance in her direction. The door clicked shut on his exit, the deadlocks automatically activated as they were designed to do.

She let out her breath in a ragged stream as she sank to the nearest sofa, her fingers going to her mouth, touching where his lips had been so briefly.

The door was locked and bolted but she had never felt more unsafe in her life…

CHAPTER SIX

GEMMA spent the next morning visiting a friend she had made from the refuge, Rachel Briggs and her little daughter Isabella. They now lived in a small rented flat in a quiet suburb just over an hour by train from the city centre.

'How is she today?' Gemma asked Rachel once they had sat down with a hot drink.

'She had another fit at about six this morning,' Rachel said. 'But she's sleeping peacefully now.'

Gemma still found it hard to believe the three-year-old tot's very own father had caused the damage that had left her suffering epilepsy from the severe fracture she'd sustained to her tiny skull. It sickened her to think that one's own flesh and blood could treat a child in such a way. The father was now serving a prison term, but it didn't seem long enough for what he had done to an innocent child. He was up for parole in a few months' time, when his daughter had a life sentence unless what Gemma had planned worked out.

'Listen, Rachel,' she said, leaning forward in her chair. 'I have a plan. I have some funds coming to me soon. It will be enough to pay for the neurosurgery Isabella needs.'

Rachel's mouth dropped open. 'I can't let you do that! It could end up costing a hundred thousand at least and that's not even counting the airfares to the States and accommodation.'

'I know all that but I'm about to inherit some money. I haven't told you this before because I didn't want you to get your hopes up, but in two days' time I will have enough money to send you to the States for as long as you and Isabella need to be there to get her well again.'

'The surgery is risky…' Rachel caught at her lip in agitation. 'There's only one guy doing it in America. What if it goes wrong and she needs to be hospitalised for months on end? It could end up costing an absolute fortune.'

'We'll cross that bridge if or when we come to it,' Gemma said. 'You *have* to let me do this,

Rachel. Please don't rob me of a chance to put right some things in my life.'

Rachel frowned in confusion. 'What are you talking about? You are the sweetest, kindest person I know. How could you have done anything wrong in your life?'

Gemma gave her a sad semblance of a smile. 'I'm not a sweet person at all. I have a past that I'm so very ashamed of. It's all come back to haunt me, but I'm determined to fix what I can. This is one way—to give little Isabella a chance at a normal life. She doesn't deserve to have her childhood snatched away from her with chronic ill health.'

Rachel's tears of gratefulness were all the reward Gemma needed. 'I can't take all this in… It's like a dream come true…a miracle…' She began to sob. 'I don't know how to thank you.'

'I don't want to be thanked. But I must insist you tell no one who gave you the money,' Gemma said. 'Please, Rachel, it's very important that you don't reveal it to anyone. It could be dangerous to you and Isabella.'

Rachel gave her a worried look. 'Because of Brett?'

'I don't want this leaked out in the press,' Gemma said. 'I come from a rich sort of background. I don't want to draw unnecessary attention to myself and thereby to you. It might get back to Brett.'

Rachel's expression became even more shadowed with apprehension. 'You think he could track me down?'

'If your name was leaked out in the press who knows what might happen?' Gemma cautioned her. 'Besides, it wouldn't do for him to find out you have money. He's due for parole soon. I know you've been relocated and all, but men like him are often very determined. He might try and track you down.'

Rachel nodded as she wiped at her eyes with the back of her hand. 'I guess you're right…but it doesn't seem fair that you don't get the chance to show the world how kind you are.'

'I'm not interested in showing the world anything. The press gave me a hard time a few years ago,' Gemma said. She paused for a moment before adding, 'Remember I told you I had an accident?'

Rachel gave a little sniff and nodded.

'Well…things are kind of complicated, but suffice it to say that I have a bad sort of reputation where the media is concerned. They would have a field-day with this, making up whatever they fancied to sell the most papers.'

'Can I at least tell my mum?' Rachel asked. 'I'll need her to come with us.'

'Your mum but no one else,' Gemma insisted. 'I don't want to put you and Isabella in any danger.'

Rachel's eyes flickered for a moment with fear. 'I know…I still live each day looking over my shoulder wondering if one of Brett's mates has been ordered to take me down on his behalf. He threatened me with it several times.'

'I know, but you can put all that behind you now. This trip to the States will be just the distraction you need.'

'I can't believe this is happening,' Rachel said. 'I never thought Isabella would have a chance at a normal life. I could never afford it and I've always been too frightened to try and go public to get any fund-raising going. You are being so very generous.'

'No, true generosity is giving something you

can't afford to give,' Gemma said. 'I can afford to give you whatever you need to help Isabella. That's not the same thing at all.'

'You are always so modest and hard on yourself,' Rachel said. 'What happened to you to make you that way?'

Gemma gave Rachel her version of a smile, but there was sadness in it. 'Experience, Rachel,' she said. 'I have learned the hard way what is important in life.'

'Yeah, well, so have I,' Rachel said with a rueful twist to her mouth. 'I stayed with Brett far too long and look what happened. If only I'd had the courage to leave the first time…'

Gemma grasped at her friend's hand and gave it an encouraging squeeze. 'Don't blame yourself. Brett was the one who hurt Isabella, not you. You did your best. Don't ever forget that.'

Rachel sighed and, lifting Gemma's hand to her face, gently kissed it. 'You have changed my life, Gemma. I feel like a completely different person since you came into my life that day I arrived at the shelter.'

Gemma fought back the tears, but Rachel's situation had always seemed so tragic and now, with the promise of hope she had been able to provide, it was all she could do to keep control. She bit her tongue and squeezed the tears back, but still they came in a stream down her cheeks. She brushed at them in embarrassment, but Rachel reached for her and enveloped her in a bone-crushing hug.

'You know, that's the first time I've ever seen you cry,' she said against her shoulder.

'I usually save it for the shower or the bath,' Gemma said, with a big, noisy sniff. 'That way I can't see how much fluid I'm losing.'

Rachel held her from her and smiled. 'You of all people deserve happiness. I wonder when it will be your turn.'

'It could be sooner than you think,' Gemma said, hating the fact that she had to act blissfully happy when nothing could be further from the truth. 'I'm getting married on Friday.'

'*Married?*' Rachel gave a gasp of surprise. '*This Friday?*'

'Yes…to a…man I knew a long time ago. It's a bit of a whirlwind romance but he has never forgotten me and, well…we're getting married.'

'Gosh, Gemma, this is rather sudden, isn't it?

Are you sure you're doing the right thing? You like everyone else at the shelter knows what can happen when women rush into relationships with men they don't know very well.'

'Andreas is not like that. He was in love with me ten years ago and came back to find me.'

'You've never mentioned him before.'

There was a lot Gemma had never mentioned to her friend before, but she didn't think now was the time to reveal all the sordid details of her past life. After all, she had only known Rachel a few months and their friendship had centred on looking after Isabella, who was so very ill much of the time.

'No, I know, but let me assure you I'm looking forward to being married to him,' she said with complete honesty, for if the ceremony didn't go ahead Isabella's surgery wouldn't either.

'What's he like?'

'Well, he's Italian and extremely good-looking,' Gemma answered, again with total sincerity. 'And he makes me feel things I haven't felt in a very long time.'

'So you love him?'

Gemma gave her a mock-reproving frown,

although her tummy did a funny sort of shuffle as she considered her friend's query. 'What sort of question is that?' she asked.

Rachel grinned. 'Yeah, well, I guess that more or less answers it. I can see you do—by the look on your face when you speak of him he has stolen your heart. Lucky you.'

Lucky me indeed, Gemma thought as she left a short time later. *It would just be my sort of luck to fall in love with a man who had re-entered my life for motives as yet unclear.*

But she had to marry him and stay married long enough in case Rachel and Isabella needed more funds.

She suppressed a tiny shiver as she boarded the train.

Six months of marriage to Andreas Trigliani.

Six long months of more secrets and lies…

Andreas waited outside for Gemma to answer her door later that day but the minutes ticked away and he couldn't help worrying about her. He'd spoken to her on the telephone earlier that afternoon suggesting they have dinner again to discuss the financial details that such a union as theirs involved. There were pre-nuptial agreements to sign, for her protection as well as his, and both of them needed to make a new will to incorporate their change in circumstances.

'Come on, Gemma,' he said out loud, leaving his finger on the buzzer. 'I know you are in there.'

Eventually he heard each lock being released and the door cracked open, but he was totally shocked by the little pale face that peered bleary-eyed from around the frame.

'S-sorry, Andreas…I don't think I can make dinner tonight. I'm not feeling all that well.'

Andreas pushed open the door once he was sure she was out of the way. '*Che cosa ti succede?*' he clipped out.

She looked at him blankly. 'Sorry, didn't understand a word of that. Can I have it in English?'

He let out a muttered curse and closed the door. 'What the hell is wrong with you?'

She put her hands to her head. 'I have a monumental headache…I get them from time to time.'

'What can I do?' His expression was full of concern, his eyes dark with worry.

'Nothing.' She shook her head then wished

she hadn't as it sent a quiver of arrows through her head. 'I just need to lie down in a dark room.'

Andreas led her to her bedroom and helped her back into her rumpled bed where she had obviously spent most of the afternoon. The blinds at the windows were down and the air was warm. He could see she hadn't had the strength to open the windows to let fresh air in.

Once she was lying down and covered with the thin sheet on her bed he went over to the window and, as quietly as he could, opened it so some air could circulate.

He stood and looked down at her white face lying against the pillow, the drawn look of her features striking a note of unease in him.

He wondered if he should call a doctor. She looked so ill he was sure it was warranted.

'Gemma,' he said softly, approaching the bed. 'What is the name of your doctor? I think you should be attended to. You look very unwell.'

She flapped her hand at him in protest, but there was no real energy in the action. 'No…please…I'll be fine. It's just a headache. I get them all the time. I've taken some strong painkillers. They'll start to work soon. I just need to sleep…'

He watched as her eyelids fluttered closed, her lips softening on a sigh as the medication started to take effect.

'Gemma?'

'I'm so tired...' She yawned like a small child and buried her head deeper into the pillow as her lashes came down, another little sigh escaping as her body finally relaxed.

Andreas waited until he was sure she was asleep before he approached the bed. He stood for a long time looking down at her, her face like an angel's, her blonde hair splayed out on the pillow like spun silk. He wanted to run his fingers through it and it took all of his self control not to reach out and disturb the slumber she needed so much.

'*Non ti ho dimenticato mai,*' he said, and then softly translated it in case some part of her subconscious could hear him. 'I have never forgotten you.'

CHAPTER SEVEN

GEMMA woke during the night with a raging thirst, but thankfully the worst of her migraine had gone. She cracked her eyes open to reach for the bedside lamp, freezing in fear when she saw a shadowed figure sitting in a chair beside her bed.

Her heart leapt upwards, her throat closing in shock, her instinctive scream blocked by sheer terror. The hand she had poised over the switch of the lamp was shaking so much she was too frightened to draw it back in case it knocked something off the bedside table and alerted the intruder to the fact that she was now awake.

The dark figure suddenly moved and she let out a strangled shriek, throwing herself off the mattress in an effort to escape and landing heavily on the floor on the other side of the bed.

'*Dio!*' Andreas's voice spoke out of the

darkness. He turned on the lamp and came over to where she was lying in a crumpled heap, fear making her eyes so wide they looked like blue-black pools of terror. 'Gemma, what are you doing to yourself?'

Gemma had trouble getting her voice to work. Her throat was tight with residual fear and her heart was still leaping all over the place. She opened her mouth once or twice but her lips were trembling and she felt as if she was going to faint.

He bent down and scooped her up as if she weighed nothing and placed her gently on the bed in a sitting position, crouching down in front of her so his eyes were more on a level with hers.

'*Mia piccola*...did I frighten you?' he asked, his features softened with remorse.

She finally swallowed the restriction in her throat and answered in a scratchy whisper, 'Yes...I didn't know who you were.'

'Do you not remember me calling on you earlier this evening?'

She put a still-shaking hand to her head. 'I had a headache...a migraine...yes...of course I remember...but I didn't know you had stayed...'

'I was worried about you,' he said. 'I didn't like to leave you on your own. I thought you might need me during the night so I brought in a chair and sat by your bed. I must have drifted off to sleep.'

Gemma looked into his dark eyes, surprised by the gentleness she could see reflected there. There were shadows beneath his eyes, indicating his sleep had not been particularly refreshing. That he had stayed with her moved her deeply. It showed a generous and kind side to his nature she had not thought possible given her treatment of him in the past. It made her feel all the more ashamed of how she was deceiving him now. She felt very tempted to confess her real motives for marrying him right there and then, telling him the truth about her infertility, but something stopped her at the last minute.

What if he didn't go ahead with their marriage because she had lied to him? He would think she hadn't changed, that she was still the selfish, stuck-up young woman of the past, out to humiliate him all over again.

She couldn't risk it, not after offering Rachel such hope. If Andreas took it upon himself to renege on the deal now everything would be lost; Isabella's only chance would be gone.

Maybe once they were married she could tell him about the little girl's situation, but not yet. Not until she had the money she needed to bring about the miracle she had prayed so hard for.

'Can I get you something?' he asked. 'Something to drink or eat?'

'I'd love a drink. My mouth gets really dry from the painkillers,' she said, wincing at the pain shooting down her leg when she tested it by moving it.

'I will get you some water.' He straightened and went towards the door.

'Andreas?'

He turned around to look at her. 'What's wrong, Gemma?'

She gave him a rueful grimace, her cheeks going a delicate shade of pink. 'Can you give me a hand to get up? I...I need to use the bathroom. I gave my leg a bit of a hammering when I fell on the floor.'

He came back over and gently eased her to her feet, his arm around her waist as he led her step by painful step towards the small bathroom across the hall. The warmth of his hand on her body made her remember the kiss they had shared and his gentle touch.

'I'll be fine now,' she said, leaning against the basin, her face now white and looking pinched all over again.

'Don't lock the door,' he cautioned. 'You could fall and I would have to break the door down to rescue you and then what would the neighbours say?'

'All right…I won't…'

'Promise me, Gemma.' His gaze was determined. 'No locked doors.'

'OK…no locked doors,' she said, wishing she'd thought to lock the door to her heart a little more securely while she'd still had the chance.

Once he'd gone to get her water she looked at her face in the mirror above the basin and wrinkled her nose in distaste at her appearance. Her hair was mussed up from sleep and the make-up she hadn't washed off before she'd gone to bed was smeared beneath her eyes like bruises, and the scar just below her hairline stared back at her with its white line of accusation.

'Please don't break on me,' she addressed the mirror wryly. 'I know this is about as bad as it gets, but the last thing I need right now is another seven years' bad luck.'

Andreas came back to the bathroom just as Gemma was coming out. 'Feeling any better?' he asked.

'I might not look it, but, yes, I do,' she said, taking the arm he offered.

'You look fine to me,' he said as he escorted her in the direction of the kitchen. 'A bit fragile, but that is understandable.'

'I don't look fine, Andreas. You're just being a gentleman. But, thanks, I appreciate it.'

He pulled out a kitchen chair for her and helped her onto it, before handing her a glass of water. He watched her drink it thirstily, her small, slim throat moving up and down like a little child's. 'More?' he asked when she'd finished it.

She shook her head. 'No, that was all I needed.'

'What about something to eat?'

'No, I couldn't.' She visibly winced. 'The thought of food makes me nauseous for a few hours after a migraine attack.'

Andreas took the chair opposite. 'How often do you get these attacks?'

'Not so often these days,' she answered. 'At first…after the accident I got them nearly every day, but they gradually lessened over time. This is the first one I've had in quite a while.'

'What do you think brought it on?'

She gave a little shrug. 'Who knows? Stress, probably. The thought of losing my father's estate to my stepmother is enough to trigger a month of migraines.'

He gave her a long and thoughtful look. 'You really hate her, don't you?'

Gemma met his eyes for a nanosecond before staring down at the empty glass on the table. It was a hard question to answer. She thought she had always hated Marcia, but now she couldn't really remember when it had started. Had she hated her before or after the accident? Gemma knew she had been a difficult stepchild for anyone to handle, and, to her credit, Marcia had at least tried in the beginning to establish some sort of relationship with her. Her stepmother's patience had however worn a little thin and it hadn't been long before things had gone downhill.

'Have you always hated her?' Andreas prompted.

Her forehead wrinkled slightly. 'I'm not sure…I guess so…'

'The stepmother role is a hard one,' he pointed out. 'I have a cousin who married a man who had two children from a previous relationship. They have made her life a living hell. They are older now but they have never really accepted her as their father's partner.'

Gemma understood perfectly; the acting out desperately unhappy children did to get attention. She saw it all the time at the women's refuge—children who were out of control in response to the emotional and physical trauma they had suffered in their lives.

She had been no different. The loss of her mother so young hadn't helped. Her father had been so absorbed in his own grief and guilt he had thrown all his energy into his work, often leaving Gemma to the care of a nanny or baby-sitter, even in the evenings when she would have given anything to be comforted by him.

When she had been old enough to go to one of Sydney's most prestigious boarding schools for girls, her father had sent her off without even bothering to disguise his relief that she was now off his hands so he could get on with his life with his glamorous new young wife.

Gemma had reacted to his rejection by deliberately causing trouble both at school and on her weekend visits home. She'd still been locked in that cycle of self-destruction when she'd met Andreas the year she'd finished school.

She had been at the hotel bored and restless for the summer holidays and festering with anger towards anyone and everyone. She had sniped and snarled at staff, even on a couple of occasions guests—which had sent her father into a totally uncharacteristic rage. He had threatened to disown her for being so irresponsible, and as she'd yelled back at him, calling him all sorts of names, he had finally lost control and told her he wished she had never been born, that she should have died instead of her mother. He had later apologised but it had been too late.

The damage had been done.

He had confirmed a belief she had carried like a heavy weight on her back all of her life.

Gemma became aware of the stretching silence

and looked up to see Andreas's steady dark gaze focused on her. She tried to conceal her reaction to his quiet scrutiny, but it was clear he wasn't fooled.

'Sometimes I wonder if in some deep part of your brain you still remember me,' he said. 'I see it in your eyes, a flicker of something every now and again, like a brief flash of recognition.'

Gemma could feel her heart begin to race as she forced herself to hold his penetrating gaze. 'I don't remember you. I'm sorry.'

'Would you like me to tell you about our...' he deliberately paused over the word '...association of ten years ago?' he asked. 'You never know, it might trigger a memory or two.'

'Um...I'm not sure it would do any good...' She looked down at her hands, agitatedly beginning to pick at a rough edge of one of her fingernails. 'The doctors said it wasn't a good idea to try and force things. They said it could be... er...dangerous.'

'I imagine it could be quite distressing to hear things that you might not want to hear,' he surmised, 'even without suffering from amnesia.'

'Yes.' She didn't look up but she was almost certain if she had she would have seen that little enigmatic smile playing about his mouth.

'It is very late,' he said as he got to his feet. 'You should go back to bed, and I need to go home and have a bit more sleep, this time in my bed instead of sitting slumped in a rickety chair.'

'Thank you for what you did tonight,' Gemma said as he came around to help her back to her room. 'It was a kind gesture. I really appreciate it.'

'It was no trouble,' he said, slipping his arm around her waist. 'I only feel remorseful that I caused you such a shock.'

'It was a knee-jerk reaction. I'm a bit nervous living on my own.'

'So that is why your front door and every window resemble a maximum security prison?'

'A girl can never be too careful,' she said. 'This is a fairly quiet neighbourhood but no one is immune to a break-in.'

'Yes, I suppose you are right. But to put your mind at ease my house at Balmoral has the best in high-tech security so you will have no need to be nervous living there. You will be completely safe.'

Not safe at all, Gemma thought as he helped her to her bed. All the locks in the world wouldn't keep her safe from the danger Andreas represented. There was danger in every touch he gave her, every probing look he sent her way, and every warm smile that melted the armour around her heart like a blowtorch on butter.

'I will pick you up in the morning if that is convenient,' he said as he pulled the sheet over her. 'We have some legal things to see to before Friday.'

'Fine,' she said, 'I'm not scheduled on at the shelter until next week. I thought since we were getting married it would be best to leave myself some time to prepare.'

'Are you sure you are all right? I can stay if you would like.'

'No, please go home and get some sleep,' she insisted. 'I'm used to being on my own.'

He gave her another one of his long, studied looks. 'When was the last time you had someone in bed with you?'

Gemma could feel her cheeks heating, but his compelling gaze wouldn't release hers. 'I hardly see that is any of your business.'

'On the contrary, I think I have a right to know

the recent sexual history of the woman I am about to marry; do you not agree?'

'I could ask the same of you, of course,' she said. 'That is if I was the least bit interested, which I'm not.'

His dark gaze glinted with a spark of anger at her pert tone. 'I do not require a performance report of each of your partners, just how long it has been since you have slept with someone.'

She moistened her mouth and answered, 'It was a fair while ago.'

'Have you had any recent medical tests performed?'

'Tests?' She disguised a nervous swallow. 'What sort of tests?'

'The usual ones you have done when you change partners. I thought I should assure you I am all clear. I had tests done recently and it would be a good idea for you to do so too, especially given the terms of our agreement.'

'I'm fine,' she said, relieved that it was at least partially true. She'd been tested for STDs after that fateful night seven years ago. She had been so terrified she might have contracted something, but she had been given the all clear then and on the repeat tests performed three months later. It seemed ironic that she had been so worried when in the end it was the accident that had ruined her chances of normal motherhood. The internal bleeding had damaged her fallopian tubes beyond repair. The doctor had delivered the news as gently as she could, suggesting the options of IVF and adoption, but Gemma had been too devastated to take much notice. She didn't feel like a real woman any more and as far as she was concerned no medical miracle technology was going to bring back what she had lost.

'Are you currently on the contraceptive pill?' he asked.

'No. I've been taking a break.'

Andreas gave her another probing look. 'No doubt this question will offend your newfound sensibilities, but it must be asked. Is there no chance that you might already be pregnant?'

Gemma stared at him, speechless.

'I realise Michael Carter could not be the father, but perhaps there was someone else?' he continued.

'There is no possible chance I could be

pregnant,' she said, looking him straight in the eyes. 'No chance at all.'

'I hope I can trust you on that,' he said.

'You can trust me,' she said, her mouth tightening. 'But if you don't I can perform a pregnancy test in front of you to verify it if you would like.'

'That will not be necessary,' he said. 'I just wanted to make sure we both are playing on a level field right from the start.'

'I understand, but I can assure you there are no cuckoos in this particular nest,' she said with increasing sharpness in her tone.

'Cuckoos?' He gave a slightly puzzled frown as if he was unfamiliar with the word.

'A cuckoo is a bird that is known for leaving its eggs in someone else's nest to be hatched and cared for by the other bird,' she explained.

'Ah, yes, *cuculo* as it is in Italian. I can see I have still much to learn even though I have spoken English for most of my life,' he said, his mouth suddenly relaxing into a wry smile.

'Your English has greatly im—' She stopped mid-word, her eyes flying back to his in case he picked up on her little slip.

'You were saying?' he prompted with a quiz- zical tilt of his head.

'I—I was saying your English has…greatly impressed me… I mean, it must be hard to switch from one language to the other, thinking in one while speaking in the other…that sort of thing.' Gemma knew she was rambling but she couldn't seem to stop, 'I'm impressed, that's all. I couldn't do it…' She held her breath, her chest feeling tight with the effort.

It was only one or two seconds at the most before he responded, but Gemma felt as if time had come to a standstill, leaving her helplessly stranded.

'If you like I could teach you to speak my language,' he offered at last. 'It is quite close to English and I am sure it would not take you long to pick up a few phrases.'

'I'd be hopeless,' she said. 'I failed every subject at school. You'd be wasting your time.'

'I am sure you are greatly underestimating your ability,' he said. 'You would no doubt be amazed at what you could do if you put your mind to it.'

'Yes, well, my mind is not what it used to be,' she responded with a little downturn of her mouth.

'You are far too hard on yourself, *cara*.'

His low, deep, gentle voice brought her head back up and her heart skipped a beat. 'That means darling…doesn't it?' she asked.

He smiled as he opened the door to leave. 'See what a fast learner you are? *Buonanotte*, Gemma.'

Gemma sank back amongst the pillows once she heard the front door click into place, but she didn't sleep another wink for the rest of the night.

She couldn't.

Her growing feelings for Andreas Trigliani kept her awake by gradually and irreversibly seeping through and filling that achingly hollow space she had carried in her chest for so long…

CHAPTER EIGHT

ONCE the legal work was dispensed with the following morning Andreas suggested they have a light lunch at his house in the harbourside suburb of Balmoral.

'Don't you have to get back to work?' Gemma asked, wondering if it was wise to spend too much time with him, especially alone.

'I have an excellent business manager,' he said. 'He will call me if there is anything that needs my immediate attention.'

'Where is your office?' she asked as they made their way to where his car was parked.

He stopped and, putting his hands on her shoulders, turned her to look back at the city outline. He pointed past her shoulder, his arm so close to her cheek she felt the soft brush of his shirt sleeve and the light lemony scent of his aftershave. 'See that that blue-glassed building, the tall one?' he asked, his warm breath gently ruffling her hair.

She could hardly breathe, let alone speak, with him standing so close behind her. The temptation to lean back against his leanly muscled frame was almost uncontrollable. 'Um…yes…I can see it.'

'I have a suite of offices on the thirtieth floor,' he said. 'But I also do a lot of work from home.' His hands fell away from her shoulders and she slowly turned around to face him.

His eyes locked with hers.

Gemma felt as if the world had come to an instant halt. The sounds of the busy city seemed to fade into the distance as she stood in front of him, looking up into his breathtakingly handsome face. Her senses were full of him; each deep throb of her heart seemed to be for him and him alone. Her hands ached to reach for him, to touch his face in a gentle caress, to explore the contours of his sensual mouth, the dark twins of his brows and the length of his aristocratic nose.

Almost without realising she was doing it she stepped half a step closer, one of her hands going to his chest to stabilise herself, the other going to his lean, cleanly shaven jaw, the softness of her palm on his masculine skin sending sparks of electricity up the length of her arm.

She couldn't stand on tiptoe without falling, but in the end she didn't need to as his head came down to meet hers in a kiss that was nothing like the soft kiss he'd given her before. There was a heated urgency in his mouth this time as it connected with hers. It was like fire meeting fuel, the eruption total and devastating.

Gemma's body sang with the rush of desire flowing through her, making her feel alive in a way she had never felt before. His arms were around her, one of his hands on the small of her back holding her against his hardening body, the intimate contact thrilling her that she had the power to attract him in spite of everything that had happened to her.

His tongue was a sweet, thrusting sword of sensuality, delving and sweeping and commanding hers into a duel that went on and on until she was consumed by the need to feel him in her most intimate place of all. She pressed herself closer, delighting in the feel of his strength and power as his mouth worked its heady magic on hers. Her breasts swelled against his chest, their tight points aching with the need to feel skin on skin instead of through the frustrating barrier of clothes.

It was Andreas who finally broke the kiss. He looked down at her up-tilted face for a long moment, his dark eyes still alight with the fire of need.

'Who started that, I wonder?' he mused with a lopsided smile.

She bit her bottom lip and lowered her gaze. 'I'm sorry. I think it might have been me...'

He tipped her chin back up to hold her gaze within the force field of his. 'Do not apologise, Gemma. You have the perfect right to initiate physical contact—after all we will be husband and wife in just over twenty-four hours.' He stroked a finger over the fullness of her bottom lip where her teeth had caught at it. 'But what I would like to know is why you felt the need to do so. Perhaps you are beginning to remember me a little, yes?'

'Y-yes...I mean no,' she said, her brain feeling like a ball of tangled string. 'I don't remember a thing...'

'You have a totally unforgettable mouth,' he

said, moving his caress to her top lip. 'I have thought of that mouth for ten years, wondering what it would feel like to have it beneath mine.'

'So…' she affected a little frown hoping it would be enough to convince him she had no recollection of that time '…have we…er…ever kissed before? In the past, I mean.'

'Believe me, Gemma,' he said with a glinting look in his eyes, 'if we had, I swear to God you would not have forgotten it.'

Gemma got in the car a few moments later, her heart still thumping erratically in her chest. She had thought it beneath her ten years ago to allow that mouth anywhere near hers. What would have happened if he had kissed her back then? Would she have still treated him the same despicable way or would she have melted into a pool of longing as she had just done?

Andreas's house was a recently renovated two storey property with a wonderfully landscaped low-maintenance garden, a lap pool and an indoor well-appointed gym, most of the rooms enjoying fabulous views over Middle Harbour.

The interior was decorated along modern minimalist lines, in muted tones throughout. The taupe large leather sofas looked luxuriously comfortable in the lounge and the entertainment system was state of the art. The works of art on the wall hinted at wealth in an understated rather than opulent way, which privately impressed Gemma.

'My housekeeper has prepared a meal for us,' Andreas said as he led her to the dining area, which overlooked the beach. 'Would you like to use the bathroom before I get her to serve it?'

'Yes…thank you…I won't be a moment,' Gemma said, finding her way back to the large bathroom on the lower floor. The walls and floor were all marbled, a big mirror above twin basins with lantern-like lights fitted into it giving the room a luxurious feel of a health spa.

She washed her hands and reapplied her lipgloss, trying to control the slight wobble of her hand as she did so.

Don't be stupid, she chided herself as she put the cap back on the gloss. *You're not alone with him; his housekeeper is here.*

She gave her blonde hair one more quick check to make sure her slanted fringe was over her scar and made her way back to the dining room.

A brown-haired middle-aged woman turned from the table as Gemma came in, her hazel eyes running over her in an unmistakably insolent manner. 'Hello, Miss Landerstalle. I am Signor Trigliani's housekeeper, Susanne Vallory. I don't suppose you remember me? I used to work for your father at the hotel.'

Gemma stared at the woman for a moment, shame rushing through her at how she had treated the cleaning staff back then. Susanne had worked her way up the ranks from the general cleaning roster to head housekeeper of The Landerstalle, but even so she had not escaped Gemma's unforgivable taunts from time to time.

'Um…yes, I do remember you,' she said, offering a hand. 'How are you, Mrs Vallory? It's been a long time and I—'

Susanne ignored Gemma's hand, her eyes glittering with mockery. 'Congratulations on your impending marriage.'

Gemma moistened her lips and dropped her hand by her side. 'Thank you.'

'I was very sorry to hear about your father's death,' the housekeeper added. 'How lucky for you, landing a billionaire just in time to inherit the hotel. Who would have thought it?'

Gemma felt the bruising blow of the house-keeper's vitriolic statements where it hurt most, but somehow managed to disguise it behind a cool, impersonal mask. 'Yes, that's correct,' she said in a deliberately imperious tone. 'The money will be mine as of tomorrow. And if you wish to continue working for Signor Trigliani in this house I suggest you keep your comments and opinions to yourself otherwise you might find yourself without employment.'

'You can't fire me,' Susanne stated. 'You've always thought you're better than the rest of the world, but, let me tell you, you're not. You're a hard-nosed little madam if ever there was one.'

'That will be all for now, thank you, Susanne,' Andreas said from just behind Gemma as he re-entered the room. 'I will serve our lunch this time. Thank you for preparing it for us. You can have the rest of the afternoon off. I will see you as usual tomorrow.'

Susanne gave Gemma one last cutting look

before brushing past, her head set at a proud, defiant angle.

'Come and sit down,' Andreas said as he pulled out a chair for Gemma. 'What would you like to drink?'

'Water will be fine,' she clipped out, still upset. 'Although perhaps you'd better check your housekeeper hasn't laced it with cyanide or something before you give it to me.'

Andreas shifted his lips from side to side in a gesture that suggested he was considering how best to go about pouring oil over troubled waters.

'Do not take too much notice of Susanne,' he said. 'She is a hard worker and does a good job for me. I am sure in time she will soften towards you.' He took the chair on her right, his long legs brushing against hers under the table.

'I doubt it.' Gemma gave him a scowl as she shifted her legs out of the way. 'Besides, she hinted she knew why I was marrying you. What have you told her?'

He met her flashing blue eyes unwaveringly. 'I told her I had never forgotten you and that we had fallen deeply in love.'

'As if she would believe that for a moment,' she scoffed. 'Besides, my engagement to Michael wasn't exactly private information. Everyone will think I'm nothing but a fickle user after all she can get.'

'I do not think it is necessary to be concerned about what other people think,' he returned. 'After all, such things did not concern you in the past, why should you be so upset now?'

'Because things are different now,' she said, fighting back tears of frustration.

'That is only because you cannot remember what you were like back then, which, judging from Susanne's reaction just now, is perhaps rather fortunate for you.'

She sent him a furious look. 'If one more person calls me fortunate or lucky I will scream. I am *not* lucky.'

'You are indeed fortunate to have the chance to claim your father's estate,' he pointed out. 'You are also indeed very fortunate to have worthwhile charity work to do and reasonable health and some measure of agility. You are much better off than many others. You should be grateful for what you have instead of burning with resentment for what you do not.'

Gemma was furious. 'Can't you see how it's all a stupid sham? Money is not what is important. It doesn't bring people back to life and it can't even change the last minute, let alone the last ten years.'

'And yet here you are agreeing to marry a man who is apparently little more than a stranger to you for the one thing you claim holds no interest to you—money,' he observed.

Gemma sat silently fuming at his cool control, which she assumed he was only exhibiting to highlight the dismantling of her own.

'It is rather strange that you remember Susanne and yet do not remember me,' he said into the humming silence. 'After all, she worked at the hotel at the same time as I did.'

Gemma felt her heart give a sudden lurch. How much had he overheard of her conversation with Susanne? Had she inadvertently blown her cover?

'Who knows?' he added. 'Perhaps spending time with her will jog your memory.'

She glared at him. 'Don't hold your breath. I

only remember her because she worked at the hotel for years.'

'Come now, Gemma,' he said. 'Have your lunch and leave your temper back where it belongs—in the past.'

'I *do not* have a temper,' she bit out through clenched teeth.

His soft chuckle of laughter flicked the hair-trigger on her control. She got to her feet and, with a savage grasp of her hand at the edge of the starched white tablecloth, cleared the table with a shattering explosion of glass, cutlery and crockery onto the tiled floor below.

Gemma stared at the seeping mess as water and the red wine Andreas had poured dripped like a fountain of blood to the floor where the remains of their lunch lay in disarray, almost unable to believe she had caused such mayhem.

He slowly got to his feet, his dark eyes smouldering with fury as they locked down on hers.

She took a step backwards, but he had already anticipated it and snared her arm, hauling her away from the mess at their feet. His fingers were like iron bands around her wrists as he counteracted her attempt to pull away.

'Let me go you…you bastard!' she flayed him.

His hold tightened, his eyes glittering danger-ously. 'Go on, you can do better than that, Gemma,' he goaded her. 'You can think of much better insults than that, I am sure.'

Gemma knew she was in unsafe territory, but it seemed as if now her anger and frustration had found an outlet it was going to be impossible to block it back up again. It was banking up inside her like a flood pushing against weakened sandbags; there was no way of holding it back.

'I hate you!' she screeched at him. 'Take your hands off me, you…you…'

'Can you not remember what you said back then?' he asked, pulling her up close, so close she could feel every hard ridge of his body against hers. 'What about the bit about how you wouldn't sleep with me even if I was the last man on earth?'

Gemma clamped her mouth shut. She couldn't allow her past to sneak up on her and take away this one chance for Isabella.

'Or how about something equally insulting about my Italian peasant body?' he continued. 'How it could not possibly bring pleasure to any woman—was that not how it went?'

She glared at him. 'How should I know? I told you I don't remember.'

He doesn't believe me, she thought in rising panic as he held her gaze, her stomach tightening in fear.

Oh, God! He doesn't believe me.

She lowered her eyes and stopped resisting his hold, her shoulders slumping, her voice coming out soft and subdued. 'If I said…terrible things like that I'm sorry… It must have been awful for you. I have no excuse for my behaviour…as you said once before, perhaps it is a mercy I can't remember…' She held her breath, mentally counting the seconds, hoping he would buy it, hating herself all over again for lying to him, but with only a matter of less than twenty-four hours until her goal could be achieved she couldn't back out now. If he were to guess she was feigning amnesia to get what she wanted he would think nothing of calling off the wedding. She was sure of it. It would after all be the perfect revenge.

Andreas gradually relaxed his hold but didn't release her. His fingers remained around her wrists, though lightly, almost like a caress. 'I should not have mentioned it, *cara*,' he said, his tone now gentle. 'It is clear it upsets you and it does no good to force things. It is over. Ten years has passed, it is not relevant to us any more.'

Gemma raised her eyes back to his, wondering how she could have misjudged him so appallingly in the past. How had she wasted her precious youth on shallow young men who had wanted her for her body and her money but not for who she really was? How had she been so blind to Andreas's highly principled and good and decent nature, ridiculing and rejecting him instead of valuing him as she should have done?

'I'm sorry…' She captured her bottom lip again. *If he only knew what she was really apologising for!*

His thumbs moved over her wrists in a back-and-forth motion that sent shivers of reaction through her body. His touch was so gentle she felt like a bruised bloom he had stooped down to pick up from the pavement, cradling it in his hand as if it were the most precious orchid in the world.

She looked into his warm brown eyes and glimpsed for a moment what she had so callously thrown away.

'Andreas…' His name was a breath of sound on her lips.

The shutters came down instantly and he let his hands fall from hers. 'I need to clean this up,' he said, turning back to the mess on the floor. 'I do not want Susanne to have any more reasons to insult you.'

Gemma made a move to help, but he waved her away with a dismissive hand. 'I will be quicker on my own,' he insisted. 'Besides—' his gaze flicked to her leg for a moment '—you need to rest your leg. You have been standing up for too long as it is.'

'But I—'

'Just do as I say, Gemma.' His tone brooked no resistance. 'One tumble on this slippery mess and you will not be able to give me what I want.'

But I can't give you what you want. She heard the words in her head but turned away before she was tempted to let them out.

Just a little while longer…

Then somehow she would find the courage to tell him.

CHAPTER NINE

ONCE the removal company had collected Gemma's things as arranged late the following morning she waited for Andreas to collect her for the ceremony.

She had dressed in a simple lightweight suit in a soft shade of pink, with a matching camisole top, and low-heeled sandals. She'd washed and dried her hair and carefully arranged it so it disguised her scar, applying just the right amount of make-up to make her feel a little less exposed.

Right on the dot of two-thirty Andreas arrived and, sweeping his dark gaze over her as she let him in, remarked, 'You look very beautiful, Gemma.'

'For a girl with a limp,' she responded deprecatingly before she could stop herself.

He paused from closing the door to look down at her. 'For your information, I hardly notice your limp. Personally, I have always considered outward beauty to be totally worthless unless it is backed up by inward grace.'

Gemma had no answer. She had hated the ugliness of her soul for so long and had tried so hard to change, but yesterday's little show of uncontrollable temper had made her realise there was still more work to be done.

'This is for you,' he said, handing her a small package. 'Happy birthday.'

Gemma stared at the neatly wrapped slim rectangle he'd placed in her hands. She had not expected anyone to give her anything, and certainly not Andreas. It had been many years since she had celebrated her birthday; mostly she tried to ignore the date as it came around each year, unwilling to acknowledge the painful memories it evoked.

'Go on, open it,' he said.

Gemma untied the little ribbon and picked at the sellotape ineffectually with her short fingernails, her hands not as steady as she wanted them to be.

'Do you need some help, *mia piccola*?'

She glanced up at him, surprised yet again at

how dark and warm his eyes were as they connected with hers. 'I—I think I can manage...I need to grow my nails...'

He took one of her hands and inspected the ragged edges, the warmth of his fingers around hers stirring her deep and low in her belly.

'You have beautiful hands, Gemma, but you are punishing them.' His thumb gently caressed the torn edge of one of her cuticles. 'You should not hate yourself so much.'

Gemma could barely breathe as he held her gaze. Her chest felt as if it were being slowly filled up with an inflatable substance, leaving no room for her lungs to expand.

'Here—' he took the package from her other hand '—I will open it for you.'

She watched as he deftly removed the wrapping and handed the velvet box back to her. She opened it to find a diamond pendant on an exquisitely fine gold chain, resting on its bed of blue velvet the colour of her eyes.

'It's...beautiful...thank you...' Her voice came out husky, a slow, seeping warmth consuming her at the thought of him taking the time to choose such an exquisite gift for her.

'I am glad you like it. Perhaps you would like to wear it now. Here, allow me to help you. The catch is very fine.'

Gemma turned as he placed the pendant around her neck, her skin lifting as his fingers touched the sensitive area beneath her hair as he fastened the clasp.

He turned her back to face him and smiled. 'It suits you. I knew it would.'

Gemma wanted to ask him what he meant, but before she could get the words out he glanced at his watch and grimaced. 'We cannot be late for our own wedding,' he said as he led the way to the door. 'That indeed would be unthinkable.'

The ceremony at the registry office was brief and largely impersonal right up until the celebrant gave Andreas permission to kiss the bride. Suddenly the atmosphere changed. Gemma could feel the build-up of tension in the air as Andreas turned towards her, his dark eyes meshing with hers as his hands went to her slim shoulders.

She held her breath as he bent his head to press a soft but lingering kiss to her mouth. She felt her love for him begin to fill her, making her chest swell as it tried to contain the breadth and width of it. She had tried her best to ignore her changing feelings, but they had resisted all of her attempts to suppress them. They flowed through her like a tide of warm water over cold river stones, heating her from the inside out. Her skin came alive at his touch, her mouth burned with the need to feel his deeper possession and her lower body started to pound with need.

He lifted his head and held her gaze for a lengthy moment, as if he was searching her soul for secrets. The pad of his thumb pressed at an escaping tear she hadn't been able to control in time, his tender touch sending more in its place.

'Do not cry, Gemma,' he said in a deep, slightly gruff tone.

'Sorry,' she sniffed. 'I'm not usually so soppy; it's just…I wish my father had been here.'

'Oh, *cara*,' he said, bringing her head to his chest. 'I am sure he is watching and congratulating us both.'

Gemma reluctantly eased herself away to look up at him, acutely aware of the interested gazes of the witnesses and celebrant standing nearby.

'I guess you're right,' she said in a lowered tone. 'At least he would have approved of you as a husband for me.'

'Even if I was not your first choice, but in fact your very last?'

Gemma wished she could tell him how much she regretted those dreadful words she'd said to him all those years ago. But until the money was in Rachel's bank account she had to remain silent. It would take a few days for the transaction to be processed and even then she wasn't sure if she would have the courage to admit to how she had lied to him.

'At least you offered to marry me,' she said with an attempt at dry humour. 'I had to bribe Michael to agree to go through with it, and even then he pulled out at the last minute. What does a girl close to thirty have to do to get a husband these days?'

There was a tense little silence as Andreas stood looking down at her. Gemma hunted his face, wondering if her glib tone had offended him in some way. 'Andreas?'

She watched as his chest rose and fell as he released a sigh before he reached for her hand

and led her out of the registry office to his car outside. 'Come, Gemma. You are looking pale and fragile. I do not want to start our marriage with you coming down with another migraine.'

Gemma felt a little crushed by his comment. Surely she didn't look that bad. Or was he subtly reminding her of his magnanimous gesture in coming to her rescue, particularly as she was no longer in robust health?

She waited until they were on their way before she glanced at him resentfully. 'You didn't have to do it, you know.'

His eyes met hers briefly. 'Do what?'

'Marry me,' she answered, turning her head away to stare out of the window. 'I still don't really understand why you did it.'

'It suited me to do so,' he said.

She swung her head back to look at him. 'I know I'm damaged goods, Andreas, you don't have to keep reminding me of it.'

His brows moved together over his eyes but he maintained his focus on the traffic. 'I can see I am going to have to work very hard to elevate your self-esteem. I do not recall at any time referring to you as damaged goods.'

'But I am, aren't I?' She didn't wait for him to respond as she continued bitterly, 'There's no point denying it. You could have married anyone you wanted and you know it.'

'But you are the one I wanted the most. I have wanted you for ten years.'

For a brief moment hope flickered and then died in her chest. *For revenge*, Gemma reminded herself. What other motive could there be? He didn't love her. How could he after what she had done?

'I told you before I am a patient man, Gemma. I have waited a long time to claim you as my own.'

'Even though you don't love me.'

'Love has nothing to do with the arrangement we have made,' he said. 'You needed a legal husband and I need a mother for my future children.'

She kept her eyes fixed straight ahead. 'What if I'm not ready to have children just yet?'

'It will happen when it is meant to happen,' he said.

Gemma looked ahead once more. What if it proved impossible? How many failed attempts would it take for him to leave her? IVF wasn't always successful and he might not even agree to it once he realised how she had deceived him.

'And if we don't succeed?' she dropped into the heavy silence that had fallen between them.

He parked his car in his driveway before answering, his dark eyes determined as they caught and held hers. 'We will succeed, Gemma. I will make sure of it.'

Once they arrived at the house Andreas noticed Gemma looking around nervously for any sign of the housekeeper. He shrugged himself out of his suit jacket, and, tossing it over the banister at the foot of the stairs, informed her, 'Do not worry. I gave Susanne the afternoon off. She will not be back until Sunday.'

She let a little sigh of relief escape. 'I wasn't sure if I was going to be up to another slanging match. I guess I must be a little out of practice.'

'I think you do quite well for yourself,' he said with a wry glance towards the dining room.

She gave him a shamefaced look. 'It won't happen again. I promise.'

He came up close, tipping up her chin to hold

her gaze. 'You have a passionate nature. I would not want you to change that.'

She ran her tongue across her lips, her heart starting to thump again. 'Wh-what would you want me to change?'

He gave a slight frown. 'What do you mean?'

'I remember enough of my past to recognise I wasn't always a nice person. Susanne's reaction confirmed it. But I have changed, Andreas. I have changed in many ways…'

His hand left her chin and was joined by his other on the tops of her shoulders. 'What has changed you, Gemma? Was it the accident?'

She held his probing gaze, all the while fighting the temptation to confess to him her sordid past. What would he think of her if she told him about her degradation? Would he be privately gloating that she had finally got her comeuppance?

'I guess I just got tired of being a spoilt brat,' she said, trying a smile, but it was twisted and sat uncomfortably on her mouth. 'It's very hard work being a super bitch, you know. I decided to take long-service leave.'

He smiled at her attempt at humour. 'And do

you plan to return to your previous post as soon as you are rested?'

She shifted her gaze slightly. 'I don't think so.'

'Because your father is now dead and there would be no point?'

'Maybe.' She lifted one slim shoulder in a shrug. 'Who knows? Perhaps I've finally grown up. Everyone has to at some stage. It's taken me longer than most but that's the way it turned out.'

Andreas looked at her for a long moment. He couldn't quite rid himself of the notion that she wasn't being entirely truthful. She was a skilled performer; he knew that from his own bitter experience. Her little I'm-nothing-like-the-person-I-was-before speech was certainly convincing, but he wasn't going to give her the benefit of the doubt.

He wanted her pride on a platter and he would have it even if it took him months to get it.

He'd already achieved his primary goal of tying her to him in a marriage she would have scoffed at ten years ago. The stuck up heiress who had made such a fool of him was now his wife.

Apart from her little temper tantrum yesterday she gave every appearance of being a reformed woman, but he wondered how long it would last. She would receive the first instalment from her father's estate as soon as the arrangements were formalised, and the final balance in six months' time along with the money from the sale of the hotel. It was in her interests to behave herself in case he put an end to their marriage before the terms of the will were met.

'We all have to face our adult responsibilities at some point,' he said into the silence. 'That is after all why I came back to Australia to fulfil my father's dream.'

Gemma looked up at him, her voice cracking slightly on the words. 'Your father would have been very proud of you. You are a nice person, Andreas. A good person.'

He gave her a crooked smile. 'What a pity you do not remember me. Perhaps I was not so nice back then, eh?'

'I am sure you were just the same as you are now,' she said, lowering her gaze to focus on the third button of his shirt. 'But perhaps I was unable to see it.'

'I have my bad side too, as do most people.'

'Maybe…but I have so many regrets.'

'Do not torture yourself with what cannot be changed, Gemma. You have the rest of your life ahead of you.'

A life without love, she thought sadly. A marriage based on a pack of lies, which she was sure was going to tumble down any time soon.

'Let us drink a toast to our marriage,' he suggested.

'Is it still a valid toast if it's not alcoholic?' she asked him.

'Of course it is,' he assured her with a smile. 'But I insist that at the very least your water has a few bubbles in it, no?'

She smiled fleetingly. The first genuine smile Andreas had seen on her face and it totally transformed her. He fought against his reaction to it, but he could still feel his heart contract and then swell until it seemed to take up all the room inside his chest. He could hardly breathe and he had to fight with himself not to show it on his face. He disguised his reaction by leading the way to the drinks bar in the lounge and concentrating on pouring her a chilled mineral water while he opened a half-sized bottle of champagne for himself. He handed her the glass and clinked it against his own.

'To the future and whatever it might bring.'

'The future,' Gemma murmured and took a little sip, adding mentally, *and whatever it might take away.*

'It is such a nice afternoon, why don't we take our drinks outside by the pool?' he suggested. 'We can even have a swim if you like.'

'I'm not much of a swimmer these days.'

'It could be what your leg needs,' he said. 'The exercise will strengthen it.'

'I don't like anyone seeing my scars.'

'I promise not to stare.'

She gave him another little shy smile. 'You're seriously tempting me.'

'That is the intention, *mia piccola*. It is hot and sticky and nothing would do us more good right now than a relaxing swim.'

She captured her bottom lip with the small white crescents of her teeth. 'I don't have a very fashionable bathing costume.'

'The garden is totally private. Just wear your underwear. Your things are in the walk-in wardrobe in our room,' he said. 'I asked Susanne to unpack them before she left.'

'I'm surprised she hasn't taken to them with a pair of very sharp scissors.'

'If she has, then I will buy you a whole new wardrobe,' he said.

To her surprise Gemma found her things neatly stored in the huge walk-in wardrobe in Andreas's room. She tried to ignore the row of his suits and casual wear as she selected what she needed from her section, tried, too, to ignore the king-size bed that dominated the bedroom.

Using the *en suite*, she changed into her only bathing costume that was both out of date and a little big for her. She hitched up the straps as best she could and, slipping on a long white cotton shirt, went back downstairs.

Andreas was already in the pool when she came outside, swimming up and down effortlessly, affecting a deft tumble-turn at each end with a fluidity of motion she could only envy.

She sat on the edge of one of the loungers and watched him, privately marvelling at his musculature as he worked his way up and down. His back rippled with cobra-like coils of muscle that had been toned to perfection, his long legs making very short work of the length of the pool.

He flipped over on his back and swam back towards her doing backstroke and she had a full view of his abdominal muscles, the tight bands standing out in ridges of steel. His body glistened with good health and vitality as he came to a stop and lifted himself out of the water, the sunlight catching the droplets and making sparkling diamonds of them all as he came towards her.

'Come in with me,' he said. 'I will help you down the steps.'

Gemma tentatively took his outstretched hand and rose to her feet, her stomach doing its own little tumble turn as his wet warmth brushed against her as he led her to the pool.

'Take it slowly,' he cautioned. 'The steps can be slippery.'

She did as he instructed, holding his hand as she went down the four steps into the cool embrace of the water. She felt it slide over her hot skin and a sigh of pure pleasure burst from her lips. 'It's wonderful.'

Andreas smiled as he let her hand go. 'This is just what you need, *cara*. It will strengthen your leg without loading it too much.'

Gemma tested her limbs in the water, surprised at how weightless she felt. For once her leg wasn't an encumbrance but acted like a ballast as she did a length of very-out-of-practice freestyle. She had to stop for a breath at the end, embarrassed that she was so out of condition.

She turned around to see Andreas's dark eyes on her and her heart gave an extra beat, which had very little to do with her physical exertion.

'Come on, Gemma,' he said encouragingly. 'Do some more. It will do you good.'

She took a breath and did another lap, feeling a little more comfortable this time as she found a kind of rhythm in her strokes. It seemed no time at all that she was at the end again and this time not so out of breath.

'You are doing very well,' Andreas said. 'Keep going.'

She gave him another little shaky smile and turned back and swam to the other end, her slim frame gaining confidence with each stroke.

A few minutes later she surfaced just beside

him, her blonde hair trailing behind her in the water. 'I can't believe how relaxing this is.'

He smiled down at her. 'You will no doubt be beating me in few days.'

'I don't think so. You look like you do a lot of this.'

'Enough to keep in shape.'

Enough to keep in incredible shape, Gemma thought as her gaze dipped to his abdomen where a trail of dark masculine hair disappeared beneath his black bathers.

'I—I think I'll do another couple of laps,' she said and pushed off from the wall.

How different he looked, she thought as she pummelled through the water. He was a man now, a full-blooded man, no longer a young boy on the threshold of manhood. His body was a power house of strength, each sinew and muscle toned to perfection.

In spite of the warmth of the water she felt her skin break out in an all body shiver at the thought of lying so close to those long male limbs tonight and for however long their marriage continued.

After a while her body declared it had had enough and she flopped to the side, her hair in tangles, her cheeks flushed and her eyes all the time trying to avoid the temptation of Andreas's body standing waist deep so close to hers.

'Had enough?' he asked.

She forced her gaze upwards and her eyes clashed with his dark intense stare and suddenly her mouth went dry, her limbs feeling as if they had run a marathon instead of done a few ineffectual laps of a backyard pool.

He reached out a hand and removed a strand of wet hair out of her face, his eyes so very dark she felt as if she were drowning in their chocolate depths. Her breathing began to accelerate, her pulses leaping beneath her skin as he reached for her, his hands on her waist possessive and yet gentle and caressing all at the same time.

His hands moved upwards to settle just below her breasts, the soft curves of her body brushing against his fingers as he brought her even closer.

'I want you, Gemma,' he said in a voice so deep she felt as if she could feel it through the sensitive layers of her skin. 'I have always wanted you, whether you remember it or not.'

She drew in a ragged breath, unable to speak as his head came down towards hers. The first touch of his mouth on hers sent her senses reeling, the first thrust of his tongue undoing her completely. She melted against him, her arms going around his waist, her hands slipping to his taut buttocks, holding him against her, the feel of his hard arousal thrilling her even as it secretly terrified her. She had never expected to feel desire so strong it would wipe away what had happened to her in the past, but she could feel it pulsing through her now, the need to feel the touch of a man with mutual pleasure in mind.

He lifted his mouth from hers to look deep into her eyes. 'I should not be rushing you like this,' he said. 'You asked for some time and I will honour that. We will not consummate this marriage until you are ready to do so.'

Gemma felt tears spring to her eyes at his consideration of her, when she had been so unforgivably harsh to him in the past. How could he find it in himself to treat her with such compassion when surely all he could remember, as she did too, was the shameful way she had made him feel ten years ago? She had accused him of a crime he of all people was not capable of committing due to his highly principled nature.

'I'm afraid I will disappoint you,' she said softly, unable to look into that dark warm gaze.

He held her close, his chest moving in and out against the softness of her breasts. 'You will not disappoint me, Gemma.'

He eased her away from him just enough to find her mouth again with his own, in a kiss so tender it struck at the very core of her in a way no one had done before. His tongue stroked along the length of hers, calling it into a dance of building desire that left her craving more of his touch. The water lapping at their bodies increased her awareness of their closeness, his thighs like a steel brace against the soft tremble of hers. One of his hands delved into the shiny wetness of her hair, the other to where her breasts were aching for his touch. When his palm cupped her through the thin worn fabric she jolted against him with reaction, her nipple so tight it felt like something between pleasure and pain. She wanted more, much more. She wanted to feel his hands on her naked flesh, touching, shaping, caressing, and his hot, tempting mouth branding her as his own.

But before she could tell him he released her

from his embrace and took a step backwards. 'You are starting to get cold, *cara*,' he said.

'I—I'm not c-cold.'

His mouth tilted at one corner as he trailed a finger down the length of her goose-bumped arm. 'You are not a very convincing liar, Gemma.'

Gemma felt her heart give a sudden kick-start in her chest as his dark, unreadable gaze held hers. 'Wh-what makes you say that?' she asked.

His smile, like his eyes, gave nothing away. 'Come inside. The clouds have taken the sun away. I will leave you to shower and make yourself comfortable. I have some business to attend to.'

He helped her from the pool with a gentle hand at her elbow and accompanied her indoors, guiding her to the bathroom before he left her to go to his study.

Gemma stood staring at her reflection for a moment, wondering if he had seen the guilt she could see written all over her face. She saw the shadow of it in her blue eyes; saw it too in the worried frown that seemed to always be between her brows.

She turned from the mirror and stepped into the shower, turning the water on full to heat her chilled flesh.

When she went downstairs half an hour later there was a note propped on the counter in the kitchen informing her Andreas had left to pick up some paperwork from his office and would return in a couple of hours. She stared at the note for a long time, wondering if he was actively avoiding her or giving her the space she desperately needed.

She let out a tiny sigh and, pocketing the note, wandered through the house, familiarising herself with her surroundings.

Each room, she decided, was like looking at a different facet of Andreas's personality. The spacious living areas with the high-tech entertainment systems indicated he liked his creature comforts, but his taste was simple and yet unmistakably elegant.

His study was lined on three sides with floor-to-ceiling books and his desk with a laptop computer positioned so that the sunlight didn't compromise the screen. She moved towards the desk where a series of photographs was arranged and picked up the first one.

It was a photograph of his family, obviously taken some time after his father had died. His sisters were very like Andreas with olive skin and dark-as-night eyes and hair. His mother was a small, elegant woman, with sharp intelligent eyes and a warm smile.

How different from her own family, she mused sadly. She had spent most of her childhood and teenage years missing her mother and punishing her father for her absence. Her strained relationship with her stepmother had only intensified her unhappiness and it had been a steady downhill run from there. Her destructive behaviour had spun out of control, leaving both physical and mental scars that she knew would never go away.

Gemma put the photo down, but her eyes were drawn to another on the desk. She reached for it with an unsteady hand, staring at the image for a very long time, a small frown bringing her brows together.

'Do you not recognise yourself from ten years ago, Gemma?' Andreas's deep voice spoke from the doorway of the study.

Gemma nearly dropped the framed portrait in her hands in shock as she spun around to face him. 'I—I didn't hear you come home.'

He entered the room, his tall figure seeming to shrink the study, which previously she had thought so commodious.

She put the photograph down on the desk, but it bumped against one of the others, sending it to the floor with a splintering of glass.

'I'm so sorry.' She stooped and began to pick up the fragments, but in her haste a shard of glass pierced her finger, bright blood spilling freely.

'*Dio!*' Andreas hauled her to her feet and, grasping her cut hand, inspected it for fragments of glass before wrapping his clean hand-kerchief around it to stem the flow of blood. 'Can I not leave you for an hour or two without you injuring yourself?'

'It's nothing,' she said, trying to pull out of his hold. 'I'm sorry about the frame; I'll pay for the glass to be replaced.'

'I am not the least bit concerned about the glass.'

A little silence swirled around them for a moment.

'Why have you got a photograph of me?' Gemma asked.

He held her questioning gaze for a long time before answering. 'I keep it as a reminder of my time in Australia. A memento, if you like.'

'It seems a rather strange souvenir, if you ask me,' she said with a guarded look. 'Most people have photos of the Harbour Bridge or the Opera House.'

'I prefer your image to that of a building or a bridge.'

She frowned at his response. 'I don't remember giving you permission to take a photograph of me.'

'But of course you do not remember, *cara*,' he said evenly. 'You are suffering from amnesia, are you not?'

Gemma was hoist with her own petard and was almost certain he knew it. She could see the glitter of something in his dark eyes and knew she would have to be very careful in future.

'That's completely beside the point,' she said. 'I just don't understand why you would want to keep a photograph of me in your collection. From what you have told me, I wasn't exactly your best friend ten years ago.'

'No, that is indeed true.'

'Then why?'

He tipped up her chin with one long finger so she couldn't escape the burning probe of his gaze. 'What does it matter why I kept it? I will throw it away if you like. Besides, I have no longer any need of it. I have the real thing now.'

His statement contained an element of arrogance that unnerved her, but she fought valiantly not to show it on her face.

Desperate to change the subject, she held up her finger still wrapped in his handkerchief. 'I need to wash and dress this.'

'But of course,' he said, leading her from the room to the downstairs bathroom.

Gemma tried not to be affected by his closeness, but her skin prickled all over as he led her to the basin and washed the wound, his touch gentle and sure. She unconsciously held her breath as he dressed the cut with a Band-Aid, his eyes coming back to hers once the task was completed.

'There,' he said. 'That should heal very nicely. I do not think it is deep enough to leave a scar.'

'That's good to hear,' she said with a wry twist to her mouth as she began to move away. 'The last thing I need is another scar.'

Andreas stalled her movement from the basin by placing a hand on her shoulder and turning her to face him. His eyes went to the white line on her forehead, one of his fingers reaching to trace it in a caress so tender she felt her heart constrict almost painfully.

'It is barely noticeable and yet you are troubled by it greatly but you really have no need to be,' he assured her.

She compressed her lips to control the emotion she could feel bubbling to the surface.

'Truly, Gemma, it is nothing.'

'Nothing?' She eyeballed him resentfully, the tenuous control on her emotions finally slipping out of her grasp. 'How can you say it's nothing? Do you know what this scar represents? *Do you?'*

'Do not upset yourself,' he said calmly. 'It will not change a thing.'

'I have permanently disabled another person,' she bit out. 'Don't tell me it is nothing. It is *not* nothing. It might not be very noticeable to you but, let me tell you, I will go to my grave with my guilt slashed permanently across my face.'

Andreas watched as she wrenched herself

from his hold and fled from the bathroom, but he didn't call her back.

He turned and looked at his reflection in the mirror and grimaced. Gemma had spoken about her guilt, but what about his own?

CHAPTER TEN

GEMMA wandered out to the garden but, as large and as private as it was, she still felt hemmed in and made her way to the street instead. She walked in the direction of the bay, the salt water smell in the air instantly lifting her flagging spirits.

She stood looking over the water as it gently lapped against the sandy shore, the sound of a boat motoring past the only sound apart from a small group of teenagers who were sitting chatting near the jetty.

How wonderful it would be to be able to rewrite the past, she thought as she glanced at their young tanned, able bodies, huddled together against the afternoon sea breeze. One of the girls laughed, the light tinkling bell sound carrying on the air striking a chord of deep sadness in Gemma's chest. The so-called friends she had surrounded herself with a decade ago had not stayed around to pick up the pieces of her shattered life. Only Michael had stood by her, which still surprised her considering she was responsible for the destruction of his life.

If only she could remember that night! Her head ached from trying to recall what had occurred before she'd left the hotel. She hadn't been drinking, but something had made her drive recklessly that night. Like her, Michael had no memory of the accident, although he'd been able to recall that Gemma had turned up at his house in an emotional, almost incoherent state after yet another argument with her stepmother.

But to Gemma it was all a blur.

A thick fog in her head that was impenetrable.

One of the teenage boys got up to throw a ball, which bounced and landed at Gemma's feet.

'Sorry,' he said, grinning at her as he bounded up to retrieve it.

She smiled at him. 'It's fine. You look like you're having fun.'

'Yeah, we hang around here a bit in the summer.'

'It's nearly over…summer, I mean,' she said shyly.

'Don't remind me,' he responded with a rueful grimace.

Gemma was struck by the likeness the young man had to Andreas of ten years ago, the lean, gangly frame; the slightly unsettled skin with the shadow of a beard that was sporadic, and the dark hair that hadn't quite made up its mind whether to stay back or fall forward.

'Are you new around here?' the young man asked.

'Yes, I just moved here today.'

'Wow, that is new.' He flicked a glance back at his friends.

'I'll let you get back,' she said, beginning to move away.

'You can join us if you like.'

'That's very kind of you but I'd better get back.'

'See you around some time,' he called out over his shoulder as he jogged back to his friends.

'Bye,' she said, feeling incredibly old all of a sudden. Had she ever been carefree and happy like those young people over there?

'Gemma?'

She turned at the sound of Andreas's voice.

She watched as he approached, his long limbs making easy work of the sand, her heart beginning to pick up its pace the closer he got.

'Are you all right?' he asked as he came to stand in front of her.

'Yes, of course.'

His eyes were very dark as they centred on hers. 'I did not mean to upset you.'

'It's fine.' She began to walk along the shore rather than meet his eyes.

He fell into step beside her but it was a long time before either of them spoke.

'Remember I spoke of travelling to Italy to meet my family?' Andreas said once they had gone the length of the bay. 'I would like to go sooner rather than later.'

Gemma stopped in her tracks to look up at him, her eyes showing her surprise. 'When were you thinking of going?'

He gave a loose-shouldered shrug. 'I have some business things to see to and my mother and sisters are keen to meet you. I thought we might go next week.'

'*Next week?*' She gaped at him.

'Is that a problem for you?' he asked.

She forced her dropped jaw back into place. 'It's rather short notice. I'd have to inform the shelter.'

'But your work at the shelter is entirely voluntary,' he pointed out. 'It is not as if you are under contract or anything.'

'No…but…'

'But?' His espresso-coffee eyes centred on hers.

'My passport is probably out of date.'

'I have already checked and it is not,' he informed her.

Gemma sent him a wary look. 'You seem to be very up to date on everything. Firstly you procure a marriage licence in less than a week, then you orchestrate legal work that would normally take a month at the least, and on top of that you have apparently done background checks on my passport. Is there anything else you have investigated without my knowledge?'

'I did some background work—yes, but only because time was short,' he said. 'I know you are short of money, that you have lived more or less from hand to mouth recently, surviving on a meagre pension from the government when a simple telephone call to your father would have solved your financial difficulties.'

She gave him an embittered glance as she resumed walking. 'You are assuming, of course, that my father would have come to the rescue. How do you know he wouldn't have told me to take a running jump?'

'Your father loved you, Gemma.'

'Yeah, well, as I said to you the other day, he had a strange way of showing it.'

'You are perhaps so like him you fail to see the impossible situation he was in,' Andreas said. 'You were coming between his wife and himself. You had done so from the first and he had to make a choice.'

'Well, bully for him. Let's hope he made the right one.'

'Your stepmother is devastated by the way the will has been written,' he said.

Gemma stopped again to look at him. 'You've been in contact with her?'

'I have spoken to her a number of times.'

A cold trickle of apprehension spilled into her veins as she stood before him. 'What did she say to you?'

'Just that she thought your father would have left something for her. She didn't expect him to give her everything, she recognised you are his only child and the rightful heir, but she was married to him for close to fourteen years, seemingly happily so. But it seemed your father was intent on a you-against-her showdown in the end.'

Gemma frowned as she considered her father's motives. Could it be he had at the last minute changed his mind about his wife? He had never believed Gemma's accounts of Marcia's behaviour towards her in the past. He had dismissed every account as nonsense and told her to grow up and get over her childish jealousy.

Her memories were fragmented, but she recalled enough to know her stepmother had eventually given up trying to be nice and instead had done her very best to undermine Gemma's relationship with her father. Marcia had been incredibly subtle about it, leaving her taunts and undermining comments until they had been alone. She had intruded on Gemma's privacy, reading her diary on more than one occasion and relaying the contents to her father with a few extrapolations of her own, making Gemma out to be a promiscuous little tramp when in fact nothing had been further from the truth. In a fit of rebellion Gemma had gone out and lost her virginity to the first boy who had shown an interest, but it hadn't been a particularly pleasant experience, and indeed nor had her other sexual encounters been anything she wanted to remember with any degree of fondness.

There had been other occasions when her step-mother had cruelly criticised her appearance, constantly suggesting she needed to lose a few pounds, which had sent Gemma into a downward spiral of self-abuse in the form of an eating disorder that had taken years to get under control.

Emotional abuse, someone at the shelter had called it.

In some ways as damaging as physical abuse, but the scars were mostly hidden.

'So why did you come to my rescue?' Gemma asked after a long silence. 'Why not side with Marcia? After all, she has by all accounts not been the bitch you intimated I was.'

Andreas's eyes moved away from hers to look out over the view across the water. 'I wanted to see you again. To see if you had changed.'

'And what is your verdict?' Gemma asked, wishing her tone hadn't sounded quite so apprehensive.

He turned to look at her, his expression revealing nothing. 'I haven't quite made up my mind. I sometimes feel you are hiding the real you from me just as you did in the past.'

She had to hide *everything* from him, that was the problem, Gemma thought. If only she could tell him the truth about her past, how she regretted her treatment of him, how she had come to have feelings for him, how she admired him for rising above their past history to come to her rescue the way he had. Sure, she suspected his motives were centred on revenge, but she knew he was still attracted to her and that gave her a thin sliver of hope that she could somehow turn things around. She couldn't give him what he wanted, or at least not naturally, but she could love him with a love that knew no bounds. Surely that would compensate for her other inadequacies?

It *had* to!

It was all she could offer him—herself.

'We should go back and have some dinner,' he

said after a short silence. 'You look as if that sea breeze is going to break you in half.'

Gemma fell into step beside him, her limp slowing them down, but if it bothered him he didn't show it. He reached for her hand and she didn't pull away as his long fingers curled around hers.

The house was like a refuge from the stiff sea breeze that had whipped up the ocean into a million galloping white horses intent on reaching the shore.

Gemma brushed her wild hair out of her eyes as Andreas closed the front door. 'Phew! It looks like autumn is on its way.'

'Do not be fooled,' he said. 'You know what Sydney's weather is like. It could well be in the high thirties tomorrow. But next week we will be in Italy where spring will be in full force.'

Gemma wanted to ask for more time before she met his family, but it seemed as if he had everything arranged. Instead she found herself discussing their flights and where they would stay as if they were any other normal married couple.

'You will get on well with my sisters,' Andreas

said as they sat sharing a meal prepared by the housekeeper and reheated in the microwave oven. 'They are very excited about meeting you.'

'What have you told them about me?'

He smiled as he reached for his glass of red wine. 'Not much, only that you are the most beautiful woman I have ever met.'

Gemma lowered her gaze to her glass of water. 'Then they will be very disappointed when they meet me face to face.'

'I do not think so.'

'Have you told them I have a limp and a scar?'

He met her defiant look with equanimity. 'I did not think it necessary to describe you in such terms.'

'How did you describe me—as a poor little rich girl with an attitude a mile wide?'

'No.'

His single-word response threw her. She sat pondering over what he had told his family, wondering if it had been flattering or closer to the truth.

'Gemma—' his voice brought her gaze back to his '—you have no need to be nervous about meeting my family. They will welcome you with open arms.'

'They will suspect our marriage is a sham.'

'Not from me,' he assured her. 'If you choose, however, to give them that impression, then I can hardly stop you, although I would advise against it. My family will draw much-needed comfort from believing I am happily settled.'

'I will do my best,' she said. 'I guess I owe you that at the very least.'

'You do not owe me anything, Gemma. No one forced me to marry you. I have done it most willingly.'

Her brows met over her eyes. 'I still don't quite understand why.'

'You do not need to understand. You are my wife and that is all you need to concentrate on at present.'

Gemma could think of nothing else. She was his wife and within the next hour or two would be sharing his bed.

As if he could read her thoughts Andreas met her eyes across the table. 'Would you prefer to spend this first night of our marriage alone?'

She ran her tongue over the dryness of her mouth, her stomach feeling hollow in spite of the meal she had just forced past her lips. 'Wwould you mind?' she said, knowing she sounded pathetically grateful but unable to prevent it.

'Not at all,' he answered. 'As I told you before, I am a patient man.'

She looked down at the tablecloth. 'It's not that you're not attractive…you are…it's just that it's been a long time since I've…slept with someone.'

'You are attracted to me, *cara*?' he asked softly.

She met his eyes once more. 'It would be pointless denying it when every time you kiss me I feel like…like…'

'Like what?'

She let out a little sharp-edged sigh. 'Like I'm alive for the first time in my life…really alive…'

Andreas got to his feet and came around to her side of the table, helping her out of her chair. He stood looking down at her beautiful face, his insides feeling as if someone had just rearranged them bit by bit. He felt empty and full all at the same time.

'If you remembered me from ten years ago perhaps you would not feel attracted to me at all,' he said after a little pause.

Gemma searched his face, wondering if he suspected her deception, but apart from a little wry smile playing about his mouth there was nothing to suggest he saw through her curtain of lies. But how could she be sure?

'Go to bed, Gemma,' he said. 'I will see you in the morning.'

'But what about the dinner things?' She indicated the remains of their meal. 'I'll help you clear up.'

'Leave it,' he said. 'You are looking pale and tired.'

'Where…where will I sleep?' she asked, tying her hands in knots in front of her.

'Wherever you like,' he answered. 'My house has six bedrooms—choose the one you are most comfortable in.'

She shifted from one foot to the other. 'Goodnight, Andreas.'

'*Buonanotte*, Gemma.' He stepped forward and pressed a soft kiss to the top of her head before moving past her, the warmth of his body brushing hers as he left the room, taking her heart with him…

CHAPTER ELEVEN

GEMMA woke several times during the night, her leg ached and she couldn't seem to get comfortable no matter what she did. Eventually she gave up and, slipping on a bathrobe, made her way out of the room she had chosen to use the bathroom down the hall.

She rummaged for some mild painkillers in the cabinet beneath the twin basins but without success.

There was a knock at the door. 'Gemma? Is everything all right?'

She straightened from the cabinet and limped over to the door and opened it. 'I couldn't sleep. I was looking for some paracetamol. Do you have some?'

'I have some in my *en suite*,' he said. 'Is your leg causing you discomfort?'

'Just a little.' She tried not to stare at his bare

chest or the black underwear he was wearing, which left very little to the imagination.

He led her to his room, instructing her to sit on his bed, which by the state of the bed linen looked to her as if he hadn't had a particularly restful sleep either.

He came back out of the *en suite* with a glass of water and two tablets. 'These should do the trick.'

She took the tablets from the palm of his hand and swallowed them with the water. 'Thank you.' She handed him back the glass and made to get up, but he placed a hand on her shoulder.

She looked up at him uncertainly. 'I should go back to my room.'

'No, do not go,' he said, his voice sounding husky. 'I too have had trouble sleeping. Stay and talk with me for a while.'

'I'm not sure that's such a good idea.' She moistened her lips nervously.

'Do you not trust me, Gemma?'

I don't trust myself, she felt like saying. 'I'm not a good conversationalist, Andreas. I would probably bore you within minutes.'

'Which is exactly what I need to help me

sleep,' he said. 'It is either that or count sheep. I have already counted several thousand to no effect.'

She couldn't help a tiny smile. 'I once counted to fifteen thousand and thirty-one, or was it thirty-two…? I can't quite remember.'

'That must be some sort of record, surely?' He smiled back as he stretched his long frame on the bed close to where she was perched, his head supported by one of his hands.

'It was when I was in hospital after the accident,' she found herself confessing. 'I was frustrated at being there for weeks. I hadn't realised what noisy places hospitals are, even in the middle of the night. I think that's why I have a problem sleeping now. It must have permanently disturbed my circadian rhythms or something.'

'Have you tried medication?'

She shook her head. 'No…I thought it best not to go down that path.'

'It must have been very confusing to find yourself injured in hospital with no memory of how you came to be there.'

'It was terrifying.' She turned to glance at him, and, after a small hesitation, repositioned herself on the bed so she could maintain contact with his warm dark gaze. 'I was so frightened. One of the police officers who interviewed me treated me like a criminal. I found out later he had lost a son in an accident so I guess that's why he was so harsh…' She caught her lip momentarily before adding, 'Not that I didn't deserve it, of course.'

'Accidents happen where it is no one's fault,' he pointed out.

'I was charged with negligent driving. It *was* my fault. There's no escaping that.'

'Michael Carter appears to have forgiven you. Is it not time you forgave yourself?'

'I'd like to be able to move beyond it one day…but I don't see how I can without remembering what led me to drive so dangerously. I wasn't even wearing a seat belt, nor was Michael, which was unusual as I am so fussy about that sort of thing normally.'

'Have you talked to your stepmother about that night?' he asked. 'Wasn't she the last person you spoke to before you left the hotel?'

She gnawed at her bottom lip again for a moment. 'Yes. I spoke to her some months after the accident. After her first visit to the hospital

I refused to see her again, which of course made my father furious. I'd asked her what we had been arguing about, but she insisted we hadn't been arguing at all.'

'But you did not believe her?'

She let out a long heart-felt sigh and began to pick at one of her reddened cuticles. 'I don't know what to believe any more. It's all like a thick fog inside my head. Sometimes I worry I might have got things horribly wrong. I read this article about Repressed Memory Syndrome, where the power of suggestion in some untrained therapists was enough to implant memories in patients which had not really occurred in real life. It worries me that what I remember is what I want to remember and not really what happened at all.'

Andreas gently eased her hand away from the damage it was doing to her cuticles and enclosed it safely in the warmth of his. 'Is that what you fell out with your father about?' he asked, his fingers moving over hers in a caressing motion. 'Your account of that night, which evidently clashed with Marcia's.'

'Yes and no.' She stretched out her legs and lay

on her side, her head like his propped up by one of her arms, her other hand still entwined with his. 'We'd always had a difficult relationship. We were both a little headstrong and I guess we both felt guilty about my mother dying.'

'You were only a ten-year-old child—surely you do not need to blame yourself for her death.'

'I know…but it's hard not to. I think of how demanding little kids can be. My mother probably put off seeing a doctor out of concern for me. I was spoilt and at times difficult to handle so finding a babysitter wasn't easy. She didn't have family close by, her parents had died and because of my father's heavy business workload she didn't have many close friends. I suppose I took my own guilt out on my father. I was a terrible daughter. I was a terrible person. My father gave me every material thing I asked for, I guess to compensate for the loss of my mother, but it wasn't what I was looking for. Looking back now I can't believe I acted so selfishly.'

'But you have changed now,' he observed, looking at her intently. 'You are almost unrecognisable from the young woman of ten years ago.'

A small silence began to tighten the air around them.

'Do you have any regrets about your life, Andreas?' she asked softly.

He released her hand and reached out and coiled a strand of her hair around his finger, tethering her to him in an intimate touch that lifted the fine hairs at the back of her neck.

'I regret not kissing you ten years ago when I had the chance,' he said, his gaze dipping to her mouth.

Gemma felt the deep thud of her heart as his gaze slowly came back to hers. 'Wh-why?' she breathed the one-word question.

He came closer and cupped her face with his hands, his thumbs rolling over her mouth until she could barely think.

'Because if I had kissed you when I first wanted to I do not think you would have said and done the things you eventually did.'

A troubled frown wrinkled her brow. 'I wish I hadn't hurt you. If I could take back the words I…' She paused in an effort to mentally screen her words in case she inadvertently revealed how much she remembered '…the words you said I said to you, I would do so in a moment.'

'You have already apologised; there is no need to do so again.'

Gemma lifted a hand to his face, her palm moving along the roughness of his unshaven jaw. 'You are a beautiful person, Andreas, a gracious, beautiful person.'

'What are you saying, *cara*?' He looked deeply into her eyes, his own glinting with something she couldn't quite identify. 'That you are falling just a little bit in love with me?'

'Maybe just a little bit,' she admitted, shivering in reaction when he kissed the side of her mouth.

The smile he gave her flipped her stomach. 'You are the most beautiful woman I have ever met,' he said just above her mouth, his weight balanced on his elbows, his legs moving to wrap around hers.

Gemma felt herself melting. She could hardly believe how much he affected her. Even the sound of his voice stirred her senses, let alone his touch. 'I want you to make love to me,' she said in a soft, breathless whisper. 'I want to be a real wife to you.'

'Are you sure this is what you want?' His eyes were very dark as they looked into hers.

'Yes. It feels right in a way that nothing has felt before. Does that make sense to you?'

'It makes perfect sense to me,' he said. 'We were perhaps destined to find each other again. It was not the right time ten years ago, but now it is.'

'Do you…' she took a wobbly breath for courage '…do you feel something for me?'

He held her gaze for a lengthy moment. 'I feel what I have always felt for you, Gemma; desire hot and strong and barely controllable. I have dreamed of this moment. I have ached for years to feel you beneath me, your breath inside my mouth, and my body inside yours.'

Gemma had no way of controlling her reaction to him. All of her senses were on fire at his touch. She felt the pounding between her thighs as soon as his erection brushed against her, the emptiness throbbing deep inside her that ached to be filled. She fought back her nervousness, but he must have noticed her hesitancy as he lifted his mouth from hers and began to kiss her neck in a series of hot little kisses that built her need for him to fever pitch. His hands gently unpeeled her bathrobe and nightwear from her;

each part of her that he exposed he anointed with a kiss that felt to her just like worship.

Her memories of her last sexual encounter faded under the gentle exquisiteness of his touch. All she felt was her need for him, her love for him rising up from deep inside, a love he hadn't said he returned, but his desire for her was compensation enough. She would hope and pray he would learn to love her as she loved him.

He ran his hand down the smooth, silky length of her thighs, trailing his fingers up and down until she was writhing with the need for more. He moved his fingers to the inner side of her thighs, moving up from her knees to the moist core that signalled her desire for him.

He parted her tenderly, his finger sliding inside with a gentleness that brought the glisten of tears to her eyes. She lifted her hips from the bed to access more of his touch, a sharp little gasp bursting from her lips when he brushed against the tender pearl of her that had swollen so delicately at his touch.

'Oh…oh…oh-h-h-h…'

The waves of release crashed over her in a tumult of feeling that she had absolutely no control over. Her body writhed and shuddered until she was completely spent, the air in her lungs coming out in a long blissful sigh as she lay back, her limbs weak, her body totally boneless.

She looked at him with wonder in her dark blue eyes. 'I didn't think…that would happen… It's never happened like that before.'

He smiled a smile that did serious damage to her insides. 'Just wait until you see the encore.'

'You mean there's more?' She tried a teasing smile, surprised at how comfortable it felt.

He brought his mouth down to hers. 'Much, much more, *cara*.'

Gemma had not thought her body was capable of more delicious feeling after what she had already experienced, but she had seriously underestimated Andreas's ability to incite her desire to even higher levels as he suckled on each of her breasts, his warm mouth a lighted taper to the smouldering fire inside her. He took his time, building her need for him to an almost intolerable level before he finally parted her thighs and prepared to enter her. She held her breath as he slid inside, gradually at first, waiting for her to grab at him, the liquid silk of her desire for him aiding his progress until he moved forward with a deep groan as if he could no longer keep control of his movements. He tried to set a gentle rhythm but it soon became more frantic and urgent in response to hers, their bodies grasping at each other with a hunger that knew no bounds. It was tender and wild at the same time, which made it all the more enthralling. It felt to her as if he was somehow intuitively aware of her vulnerability and was fighting with himself to keep check of his movements. But it was as if her body had somehow recognised his as the one to give her the freedom of pleasure she had been denied in the past and it urged him on without restraint.

Andreas heard her high cries just as his final plunge took him to the paradise he had dreamed of for a decade, his body exploding with the power of it, anointing her intimately with his life force.

He lay above her, unable to move, not wanting to break the union that he had craved so long.

He suddenly became aware of something wet dripping onto his arm where Gemma's head was turned and realised with a shock she was silently crying.

'*Dio Mio!*' He lifted himself off her and tenderly brushed at the tears that were falling from her eyes. 'I have hurt you?'

She shook her head, her bottom lip still trembling even though her teeth were once again trying to control it. 'No…you didn't hurt me.' She gave a tiny movement of her mouth that looked like a smile and added, 'You did the very opposite. You healed me.'

He frowned in puzzlement. 'I do not understand.'

Gemma found his tone so soothing and compassionate she found herself spilling out the painful details of the night that had changed her life. He listened, his expression showing first his shock, then his anger and his empathy that she had suffered at the hands of an unscrupulous man who had not been served the justice he deserved.

'I haven't been able to…to…become intimate with anyone since,' she confessed. 'You're the first man I've even kissed since…that night. It seems ironic in a way that it's my birthday. Seven years ago almost to the hour I had just experienced the most degrading experience of my life and yet you have turned it around, making me feel as if that terrible thing has no power over me any more.'

Andreas felt as if his chest had been crushed with a heavy weight. Her dark blue eyes were full of pain at recalling the memory. How ironic that she had totally forgotten him but recalled the fiend who had degraded her so?

Andreas wasn't a violent man, but he felt as if he wanted to find justice for her. To track down the man who had crushed her beyond recognition and beat him to a pulp for what he had done to her.

'It must have been a lesson I needed to learn,' she said into the aching silence.

'No!' He held her close, his chin on the top of her head, her body cradled in the strength of his. 'No woman deserves to be treated in such a way.'

'I was drunk,' she reminded him with another deep pang of shame. 'I wasn't in control of myself and I should have been. I had never been quite so drunk before.'

'No matter. That is no excuse. No one should take advantage of anyone who is unable to give proper consent,' he insisted.

Gemma shifted so she could look into his eyes. 'I have never met anyone like you before.'

Andreas had shown emotion only twice in his adult life. The first time Gemma had missed it by mere seconds, the second had been at his father's funeral where the weight of family responsibility combined with his loss had broken his normally steely control.

But somehow seeing the simple trust in Gemma's eyes as she looked up at him now broke through to where he had sworn no one would ever go again.

He felt the ache behind his eyes and had to look away in case she saw how she had moved him.

He didn't want her to move him.

He had no plans to allow her love to get under his guard. He wanted to stay emotionless, to teach her a lesson for her past behaviour. Besides, what if it was all an act? How could he be sure? He had been so certain of her attraction to him ten years ago and look how that had ended. With one bare-faced lie she had ruined his chances of making it in Australia under the tutelage of her father. It had taken him years of back-breaking hard work to repay his family's debts and to this day he couldn't help blaming her for his father's untimely death.

'Andreas?' Her voice was a soft whisper, but he resolutely ignored it as he moved off the bed and reached for his bathrobe, tying the ends with unnecessary force.

'I need a shower,' he said, moving towards the *en suite*. 'I will leave you to sleep the rest of the night in peace.'

Gemma frowned as the *en suite* door closed behind him, her spirits instantly plummeting. She couldn't help wondering if he was disappointed in some way. She had shared her heart with him and it had repulsed him, maybe just as her body had done, just as it repulsed her every single day.

The scars on her leg and face were bad enough, but she was carrying less weight than was ideal for her height. He was probably used to women who had more to offer in terms of looks and personality, glamorous women who were happy with casual encounters without serious long term commitment.

She wondered if perhaps he was regretting

their marriage now it had been consummated. The desire he'd said he'd felt for her for ten years was now finally slaked. After all, wasn't that why he had married her in the first place; to seek revenge for how she had treated him in the past? To own her. To show her that she needed him. Her rejection of him had rankled so much he had married her to achieve that which he hadn't been able to do before.

No doubt this was the price he had planned for her to pay. To get her to fall in love with him only to walk away as she had done to him, her crushed pride his final trophy.

She knew it was what she probably deserved but still she longed for a second chance. A chance to rewrite the past and show him the respect and love she should have shown him the first time around.

He was right—one kiss might very well have changed the course of her life.

She closed her eyes with a sigh.

One kiss and fate might have written another completely different path for her to follow…

CHAPTER TWELVE

WHEN Gemma woke the next morning Andreas was already up and about, showered and looking very fit after a strenuous workout in the gym. She could see the bunched muscles in his arms as he poured coffee from the pot as she came into the kitchen.

'I have organised our flight for Naples,' he informed her after a brief greeting that seemed to Gemma to be somewhat distant and formal. 'We leave on Friday morning.'

'So soon?'

He glanced at her as he put the coffee pot down on the bench. 'Do not worry, Gemma. The money will be in your bank account by then.'

She frowned at the cynicism in his tone. 'It's not just about the money.'

His dark brows rose slightly. 'Is it not?'

'Of course not.'

'It seems to me you have gone to extraordinary lengths to secure a veritable fortune, which you keep telling me is of no significance to you.'

'I told you I need to pay some bills.'

His frown deepened. 'So you are still keen to sell the hotel?'

'Yes.'

'For what price?'

She gave a dismissive shrug. 'I have no idea what it is worth. I'll leave it to you to decide.'

'You are being very unwise in trusting someone you hardly know to handle such a large amount of money,' he said. 'How do you know I will not swindle you?'

Gemma met his gaze directly. 'You're not that sort of person. You're a businessman with principles. If you weren't you wouldn't have achieved all that you have achieved.'

'I still think you should think about this for a few days before you make your final decision.'

'No,' she insisted. 'I've already made up my mind. The first instalment is not enough for what I want. I will need the proceeds of the hotel sale in six months to give me the financial security I desire.'

He gave her a dry look. 'Just how many credit card bills have you got piled up?'

'Enough to keep me awake at night,' she answered.

'Have you not heard of budgeting?'

'Look, I don't need a financial planning lecture, Andreas,' she said. 'I haven't been able to work due to my injuries so don't harp on at me about being useless with money. I haven't bought a thing for myself in ages.'

'I have noticed that about you,' he said. 'Your clothes are hardly what one would call fashionable.'

'I'm not interested in being fashionable.'

'You were noted for it in the past,' he reminded her. 'You only had to wear a certain colour or a certain style and it became *de rigueur*.'

'Yes, well, that was then, this is now. I'm not comfortable in bright colours and flashy designs.'

'Because of what happened the night of your twenty-first birthday party?'

Gemma's eyes shifted away from his. 'Don't make me regret telling you about that night. I would prefer it if you would not refer to it again. It has taken me many years to ease the pain of it. It won't help me if you keep bringing it up.'

'I am sorry.' His tone immediately softened. 'I will not mention it again.'

'Thank you.'

'I have some work to see to before we leave on Friday,' he said into the little silence. 'Will you be all right here on your own for the rest of the day? I am sorry, but there are things I have to tie up with my business manager in order to take ten days' leave.'

'I am used to being alone. Please don't worry about me, I prefer my own company anyway.'

Andreas looked at the downward turn of her mouth and fought against his sudden need to haul her into his arms and offer her the comfort it was clear she needed, but he knew by doing so he would be drifting into dangerous territory.

He still didn't quite trust her.

His instincts told him to keep her at a distance even as his heart struggled with the cost to him personally.

He could feel the gradual reawakening of the feelings he'd had for her ten years ago even though he had done everything he could to ignore them. Sleeping with her had only made it a hundred times worse.

He did not want to fall in love with her again. For all he knew she could be setting him up for the destruction of his pride all over again.

Gemma had taught him well.

He had not felt a thing for any of his previous lovers, always keeping himself at a safe distance, responding physically but without the complication of emotion.

Gemma stirred him in a way he had not expected after all this time. Her fragility and vulnerability had triggered his instinctive need to protect and guard those under his care. She was under his care and protection for the time being, but it didn't mean he had to fall in love with her.

That was for fools who were unable to learn from their previous mistakes.

He was not a fool.

And he was not going to give her another chance to make him one.

Gemma decided to visit Rachel and Isabella rather than spend the morning alone. But when she arrived at her friend's house she was shocked to see how upset Rachel was when she opened the door to Gemma's call.

'What on earth's the matter?' she asked as she took the fractious Isabella from Rachel's arms.

Rachel scrubbed at her cheeks, her hands visibly shaking. 'I think someone's been following me.'

Gemma felt her stomach drop. '*Oh, no!* Have you called the police?'

Rachel shook her head. 'No, I don't want to draw attention to myself. If a cop car turns up here what will the neighbours think?'

Gemma frowned at her friend's skewed reasoning even though she could understand why Rachel felt the way she did. Rachel had had a difficult time convincing the authorities in the past about her partner's behaviour; even some of her neighbours had denied hearing any of the violent episodes that had gone on until she had finally found the courage to leave.

'Look, the money should be processed in the next few days,' Gemma did her best to reassure her. 'You'll soon be safely in the States away from all of this before you know it.'

'I know.' Rachel rubbed at her arms agitatedly. 'I just can't help feeling as if something or someone is going to snatch this chance away from Isabella.'

Gemma gave Rachel a fiercely determined look as Isabella snuggled close to her neck, the little sobs now reduced to soft little hiccups as she stroked the little tot's back. 'Nothing is going to take away Isabella's chance,' she said. '*Nothing*. I won't allow anything or anyone to stand in her way. I can book the tickets for you to save time, then all you have to do is pack and get on that plane.'

Rachel bit her lip. 'I'm probably being paranoid. I know Brett is locked away but I felt sure someone was watching me when I came out of the post office yesterday.'

'Maybe they were looking at how cute Isabella is,' Gemma suggested, trying to allay her friend's fears. 'Isn't that right, gorgeous?' she cooed to the little child in her arms. 'Who could walk past you and not want to pick you up and cuddle you?'

Rachel smiled, her tense shoulders beginning to relax. 'She is adorable, isn't she?'

Gemma smiled over the top of Isabella's head. 'She's the most precious little girl in the world.'

Rachel reached out a hand to touch Gemma's

arm. 'Thank you, Gemma. I know I said it the other day, but even if I say it every day for the rest of my life it's never going to be enough to thank you for what you've done for us.'

Gemma concentrated on Isabella's little fist, which was doing serious damage to one of her earrings. 'I don't want to be thanked. All I want is for Isabella to get well.'

Rachel reached for her daughter and cuddled her close. 'Then that's what we'll aim for and God help anyone who stands in our way.'

When Gemma returned to Andreas's house she was surprised at how slowly the rest of the day passed without him around. She filled in the time the best she could, but she was restless and bored for the greater part of the afternoon.

She spent a short time in the pool, testing her strength, enjoying the exercise and the comfort it offered to her damaged leg. She wondered if she was imagining it, but each lap she did she felt a little stronger, the muscles responding with an energy and vigour they hadn't felt in years.

The sun was fiercely hot and finally forced her indoors, where she spent a miserable hour or two trying to read a book she really had no interest in, in spite of its best-selling status. She eventually tossed it aside and wandered into the kitchen where she lost herself in preparing a meal.

She had done a cooking course a couple of years ago and relished the art of preparing ingredients into a nutritious meal. Andreas's kitchen was well stocked with fresh and store-cupboard ingredients so it was relatively easy to prepare a rich beef casserole with vegetables and a passionfruit flummery for dessert.

The telephone rang just as she was trying to find a place in the refrigerator for the dessert, so she left it on the bench and reached for the extension.

A woman's voice spoke on the other end in a sexy purr, 'Hi, Susanne. Is Andreas about?'

'This is not Susanne,' Gemma said stiffly.

'Oh? Who are you—a new housekeeper?'

Gemma felt herself bristling. 'No, I'm Andreas's wife.'

There was a short silence at the other end.

'Can I take a message for you?' Gemma finally asked. 'My husband is not at home at present, but will be back shortly.'

'No, I'll speak to him personally when he gets here,' the woman said with grating confidence. 'We're having dinner together this evening— didn't he tell you?'

Gemma felt like throwing the passionfruit dessert at the nearest wall. 'He mentioned something about some tedious business matters he had to see to,' she responded with a bitchy tone she abhorred using, but something about the woman's attitude irked her immensely.

'So you are the infamous Gemma Landerstalle,' the woman said. 'I've heard all about you. I must say it didn't take much for Andreas to get your fiancé to change his mind about marrying you.'

Gemma felt her skin begin to prickle all over. 'What do you mean?'

The woman gave an amused chuckle. 'Andreas paid him to jilt you at the last minute. Didn't he tell you? He offered him three times what you were offering and your fiancé took it.'

Gemma felt as if something cold and hard had just been dropped into her stomach. It was all she could do to remain in control as her whole body began to shake with anger. 'I don't believe you.'

'No, I guess not, but you have only to ask that new husband of yours. It's not as if he has to keep it a secret any more. He's got what he wanted. You've promised him the hotel, haven't you? That's all he ever wanted and he was prepared to marry you to get it.'

Gemma could barely think, let alone speak, but somehow she managed to get out through stiff lips, 'Whom shall I say called?'

'Ah, I hear him now,' the woman said. 'He's just arrived. Looks like you will have to take second place tonight. But then in Andreas's mind business always comes first, but then he knows all about pleasure as well. I know it from personal experience.'

Gemma wanted to have the last word but the phone call was cut off before she could get the words past her tight, aching throat.

Anger rushed through her like a hot red tide. Not only had Andreas bribed Michael into letting her down so he could swoop in for the kill, he also had a mistress. He was with the woman now, so soon after sleeping with Gemma.

It was the cruellest betrayal of all. She had revealed her vulnerability to him. She had told him she was starting to fall in love with him and he had gone from their union to another woman's bed as if her confession had meant nothing to him.

It *did* mean nothing to him, she reminded herself painfully. What she had always suspected was true. He was after revenge and he had surely achieved it. She had let her guard down for the first time in her life and he had exploited her in the most despicable way possible.

It didn't matter that a part of her felt she deserved it. It hurt too much to consider he had the perfect right to inflict a portion of the hurt she had inflicted on him.

She loved him.

Nothing could change that.

It was an immutable fact.

She loved him in spite of how he had exacted revenge, but she knew he would have to work very hard to keep that hurt a secret from him.

Gemma heard him come home in the early hours of the morning, the jangle of his keys hitting the hall table before he moved up the stairs with his unmistakable tread.

She wanted to fling herself out of the spare bedroom and throw every burning accusation she had been rehearsing for hours, but instead she lay stiffly in her bed, her eyes clamped shut, her body in a tight ball as she heard him move through the house.

She heard him stop outside her door, but he didn't knock on it or open it. After a few moments she heard him move away again and she let her breath out in a ragged stream that scored her chest.

When she woke the next morning after a fitful sleep Andreas had already left for work and Susanne was cleaning the kitchen, sending Gemma a caustic look as she came in.

'If you must play in my kitchen in future please clean up after yourself,' Susanne said. 'It's taken me the best part of an hour to get this place back in order.'

'It's not *your* kitchen,' Gemma shot back.

The other woman's lip curled. 'It's not yours either, or at least it won't be for any longer than six months. That husband of yours won't take long to see you for who you really are. The honeymoon is already over as far as I can tell.'

Gemma was almost speechless with shock at the housekeeper's words. But then she recalled how many times in the past she had made cutting remarks about the staff, including Susanne, and realised she would only make things worse by entering into a no-win sparring match.

She pushed what remained of her pride to one side and met the housekeeper's blistering glare with a humble, beseeching look. 'Mrs Vallory… Susanne…I realise I have been a horrible person in the past… I have no excuse for my behaviour. I know you won't believe me when I say I've changed, but I have. I want to apologise for the hurt I have caused you, I know I was rude to you on more than one occasion, as indeed I was rude to most of the staff. I have many regrets about the way I have behaved. It was selfish and immature and caused everyone unnecessary hurt and I'm deeply sorry.'

There was a heaving silence.

Gemma searched Susanne's face for a softening of attitude, but it seemed as if one apology was not going to be enough. The housekeeper gave her a disparaging look and continued scrubbing the bench.

'We'll see,' she said, her lip still curled disdainfully. 'It was a very pretty little apology but words are not what count in my book.'

'You're right, of course,' Gemma said. 'Actions speak so much louder. I have a lot of work to do to repair the damage I've caused... some of it I can never undo and I have to live with that. My biggest regret is I didn't say what I needed to say to my father. I never told him I loved him, but I did—desperately. I guess that's why I was always trying to get his attention, to make him notice me.'

Susanne looked up from her scrubbing for a moment. 'Your father should have spent more time with you,' she acceded gruffly. 'I'm divorced now but I have a daughter of fourteen. The one thing she craves is time with her father and it's the one thing he won't give. Too busy with his new partner and work and so on.'

'What is her name?' Gemma asked as she pulled out a kitchen stool to sit on.

'Joanna,' Susanne answered with a proud maternal set of her shoulders. 'She's a spirited little thing, but far too sensitive for her own good.'

'I know how that feels,' Gemma confessed

with a sad little sigh. 'It's all an act, you know, the brash exterior to cover the inner insecurities.'

There was another tiny silence.

'Would you like me to make you some breakfast?' Susanne asked. 'I can whip up some pancakes or an omelette?'

'Oh, no...please don't bother. I'm not hungry anyway.'

Susanne gave her a reproving look. 'Didn't your mother ever tell you how breakfast is the most important meal of the day?'

Gemma's mouth twisted sadly. 'I guess I must have been too young to have heard her say it...'

The housekeeper's hand came down over Gemma's on the bench and gave it a tiny, almost imperceptible squeeze. 'I'm sorry, that was insensitive of me. I forgot you lost her so young. A ten-year-old girl needs her mother to prepare her for womanhood. It's no wonder you had a hard time coping.'

'You're not the one who should be apologising to me,' Gemma insisted.

'There are always two sides to every story,' Susanne said. 'I can see that now.' She offered her hand across the bench. 'Truce?'

Gemma took Susanne's hand and grasped it firmly. 'Truce.'

Susanne's face broke into a friendly smile. 'I was impressed with that dessert you made, by the way. You must give me your recipe. Where did you learn to cook like that?'

'You mean you didn't throw it out?'

Susanne gave her a sheepish look. 'I seriously considered it, but it looked too delicious to toss away. Besides, you've saved me a couple of hours' work on tonight's meal. The casserole you made will be all the tastier now the flavours have matured.'

Gemma's mouth turned downwards. 'That's if Andreas is free tonight.'

'Look, Gemma, since we're being honest here, I don't know what Andreas's motives were for marrying you, but he's a good man. Your father liked him immensely. I know you suffer from memory loss since your accident, but Andreas was in love with you ten years ago. He was totally besotted with you. He would have walked around the world a hundred times to claim you as his own. We all thought it was terribly sweet at the time. He was so young and a bit wet behind the ears, if you know what I mean.'

'I treated him appallingly.'

Susanne's forehead wrinkled in a puzzled frown. 'But he told me you didn't remember him, that you didn't even remember what you'd said about him that last day.'

'Um...I—I don't.' Gemma hated lying but knew she had no choice. 'But I assumed from your reaction the other day and things he's said that he didn't escape my atrocious behaviour.'

'Well, he must have forgiven you, otherwise why would he have married you?'

For revenge. Gemma almost said the words out loud. 'He has a mistress,' she blurted instead. 'I spoke to her last night.'

'Then you'll have to try even harder to convince him you've changed,' Susanne advised. 'He's not going to allow you to get another chance to hurt him. Men hate being made vulnerable, especially men like Andreas.'

'I know,' Gemma said with another sigh. 'I didn't realise loving someone could hurt so much.'

'You love him?'

Gemma nodded. 'As soon as he kissed me something inside of me shifted… I've never felt anything like that before.'

Susanne took her hand again and gave it another gentle squeeze. 'You really have changed, haven't you?'

Gemma met Susanne's motherly gaze and felt something warm and liquid seep into the cold loneliness of her body. 'It's taken me a long time, but, yes—I have.'

'Then all you can do is be yourself and hope that Andreas falls in love with the new, reworked version of Gemma Landerstalle.'

Gemma gave her another crooked smile. 'I'm still a work in progress. It could take me years to perfect it.'

'You are perfect just as you are,' Susanne said, unwittingly giving Gemma the biggest compliment of her life. 'You have a heart, Gemma. I didn't think you did, but you have.'

But it's very likely to get broken beyond repair, Gemma reminded herself as she took the cup of coffee the housekeeper had poured for her.

'To second chances,' Susanne said as she clinked her mug against Gemma's.

'To second chances,' Gemma responded. *Even if I don't really deserve them...*

CHAPTER THIRTEEN

'WHAT do you mean there's a problem with the estate?' Andreas asked his business manager, Jason Prentice. 'I thought the will was straight-forward.'

'It is more or less, but there are some last minute complications.'

'What sort of complications?'

'Marcia Landerstalle is contesting her husband's will,' Jason informed him. 'The legal eagles won't release the funds to Gemma until the courts have thrashed it out.'

'But Gemma has been named the principal heir,' Andreas said. 'And she has so far fulfilled the terms laid down by her father.'

'I know, but you know what lawyers are like— they like to prolong these sorts of things so they can extract as much money as they can from their clients. Even if you engage the best legal team you can Marcia Landerstalle has enough family money of her own behind her that could make this go on for months, maybe even years. Contestations of wills often do, so much so that there's often very little left of the original estate when a final decision has been made. Mrs Landerstalle has engaged one of Sydney's top lawyers and, believe me, with the reputation he has, the fight could get very dirty. I know wills are generally hard to contest, but the way this one is written is open to all sorts of interpretations. And it certainly doesn't help Gemma's cause to have been estranged from her father for over five years.'

Andreas let out a hissing breath. 'Gemma is not going to like this.'

'No, I guess not,' Jason said. 'But what surprises me is why Marcia Landerstalle didn't start this earlier.'

Andreas rubbed his jaw as he thought about it. 'She probably did not think Gemma would ever marry. Besides, we kept it from the press. Marcia may have only just heard of it.'

'Mmm, that makes sense, I suppose,' Jason said. 'Anyway, I would suggest you pay off your wife's debts for the time being and wait until the lawyers thrash it out. A man of your means can surely cope with a few credit-card statements.'

'Gemma wants to sell the hotel to me.'

'Really?'

Andreas nodded.

'For what price?'

'She's leaving that up to me to decide.'

'Well, she hasn't the authority to sell it to anyone until it is officially declared hers.'

Andreas drummed his fingers on the desk for a moment trying to get his head around this new development. Gemma had only married him to access her father's estate and now that access might not occur for months on end, perhaps even years. He hadn't intended staying married to her for longer than a year, eighteen months at the most. He'd told her he wanted a child as a test to see how far she was prepared to go to achieve her ends, but knowing Gemma as he had ten years ago she would willingly hand the infant over if he offered her enough money. Money was the language she'd grown up with. Why else was she so determined to have her father's estate? She hadn't spoken to her father in over five years, but it hadn't stopped her going to extraordinary lengths to gain access to his fortune.

'Is there anything else I should know about?' he asked his business manager.

'Yes,' Jason said, 'but good news this time. The property you were interested in on the central coast is available. The vendor has agreed to accept the offer you made. The development can go ahead once we get planning approval.'

'Anything else?'

'No, just the usual paperwork,' he said, running a hand through his sandy-blond hair. He glanced at his watch and added, 'This lot is going to keep me away from my wife's parents' anniversary celebration.'

Andreas lay a hand on his shoulder as he made a move to leave. 'You have done a good job as usual, Jason. Go home and relax. I am sorry I had to put all this on you at short notice but with this trip back to Italy I had no choice. I need to leave you in command.'

'It's no problem,' Jason said. 'The thought of spending three or four hours with my in-laws wasn't all that attractive anyway.'

Andreas smiled. 'Call me if you need me. You can reach me at any hour on my mobile.'

'I hope it goes well with your trip, Gemma meeting your family and all.'

'I am sure my family will adore her instantly,' Andreas said.

'I'm sure they will,' Jason said. 'She's a beautiful-looking woman, or at least she was when I last saw her.'

Andreas frowned. 'You've met Gemma before?'

'Yeah, didn't I tell you I worked at one of the nightclubs near The Landerstalle a few years ago? I'm not sure if it was the same time you were in Sydney or not. Gemma had a bit of a party-girl reputation back then. Then all of a sudden she pulled out of the social scene completely. Became a sort of recluse, I heard.'

'Maybe she just grew up,' Andreas suggested.

'Yeah, well, we all have to some time, I guess,' Jason said, picking up his folder of paperwork.

'Yes…yes, we do,' Andreas agreed as he followed his manager out of the office and closed the door with a little frown setting between his brows.

* * *

'Where's Susanne?' Andreas asked as he came into the kitchen later that evening where Gemma was keeping a careful eye on the reheating of the casserole she'd made the day before.

'I gave her a couple of hours off.'

Andreas raised his brows. 'And she agreed?'

'Yes.'

His eyes went to the meal she was assembling. 'What are you doing?'

'What does it look like I'm doing?'

'I employ Susanne to prepare my meals. I do not expect you to do so.'

'No, I'm just the woman you sleep with as a one off before you head off to your mistress,' Gemma said through tight lips.

She saw him stiffen, his jaw so tight that his lips looked white-tipped at the corners.

'Would you care to explain that comment?' he asked after a tense silence.

'I don't see the need to do so,' she returned. 'You can do what you like with your private life, which means of course so can I.'

'I do not have a mistress.'

'Then perhaps you should remind the woman who called yesterday evening asking to speak to you. She was under the impression she was your current lover.'

'What was her name?'

'She didn't say. Besides, I didn't get the time to ask as she cut the call short when you arrived at her house for dinner.'

'I had dinner in my office.'

'Nice try, Andreas,' Gemma said with her hands on her hips. 'But I'm not so gullible. Don't get me wrong, I'm not the least bit jealous. You can see whomever you like, but I would appreciate it if you would at least be discreet about it.'

'What sort of man do you think I am?' he growled.

Gemma met his brooding gaze. 'I don't really know, do I? I thought you were a man of principles, an honest, decent man, and yet you apparently think nothing of carrying on an affair behind my back.'

'I am *not* carrying on an affair behind your back.'

'No,' she said, scooping up the casserole with pot holders to take it through to the dining room, 'you're doing it right under my nose.'

Andreas let out a rough curse and followed her

through to the dining room. The table was set beautifully and he felt himself backing down. It was clear Gemma had gone to a lot of trouble in spite of what she believed he had done to betray her.

He couldn't make her out. Why tell him she was developing feelings for him only to insist she wasn't jealous?

Unless she had an ulterior motive…

He took the seat she had assigned him and picked up the bottle of red wine she'd corked and allowed to breathe and poured out a glass.

'I have some rather unfortunate news to relay to you,' he said once she had dished out their meal.

'Oh?' She gave him a glittering glance. 'Is this where you finally confess to me how you paid Michael not to marry me?'

He met her fiery look without flinching. 'I was going to leave that until later, but now that you have mentioned it perhaps I should explain my motives.'

'I would appreciate it, late though it is,' she returned with a diamond hard flash of her blue eyes.

'You were on a pathway to destruction. I wanted to counteract it.'

'Well, thank you so much for stepping into the

breach like that,' she said with heavy sarcasm. 'I really don't know how to thank you.'

'He was not the right husband for you.'

'And you are?' She gave him an incredulous look. 'Please, I might have lost part of my memory, but I'm not completely brainless.'

'I did not want you to throw your life away on a man your father did not feel confident would have your best interests at heart.'

'I hardly see that you are any improvement on Michael,' she said bitterly. 'You've already betrayed me, not once, but twice.'

'Your father did not trust Michael Carter.'

'My father was bigoted about Michael's life-style. He didn't stop and think for a moment about how Michael had stood by me when everyone else had left me to cope with my injuries alone.'

'Guilt has a habit of doing that.'

Gemma frowned. 'What do you mean by that?'

Andreas let out a long-winded sigh. 'You have so readily accepted the blame for the accident, but have you ever considered you might not have been responsible for what happened that night?'

She stared at him for what seemed like endless

seconds. 'I—I don't know what you mean... They did DNA testing. It was my car, I was driving...my fingerprints were all over the steering wheel.'

'You remember nothing of that night. How do you know it was as it was reported?'

She lowered her gaze to the food on her plate. 'I just do. It makes sense in a way—call it karma or whatever, but I had it coming to me. I deserved it.'

'I do not think you deserve to punish yourself indefinitely with something you have no memory of. We *are* our memories. If you wipe the slate of someone's brain they cease to be the person they once were.'

She frowned as she took in his words. Could it be true? Could you really change the past in such a way?

'So...what you're saying is the Gemma Landerstalle of ten years ago no longer exists?' she ventured.

'Who knows?' he asked. 'What do you think? You are the only one who can really answer that truthfully.'

She looked down at her plate once more. 'You said you had some unfortunate news to relay to me. What did you mean?'

'It is bad news.'

She looked up at him. 'You're having more than one affair?'

He gave her a rolled-eyed look. 'No, much worse than that I am afraid.'

Gemma felt her stomach free fall. 'Wh-what sort of bad news?'

He met her worried gaze across the width of the table. 'Your stepmother is contesting your father's will.'

She swallowed convulsively. 'But I'll still get my money in the next couple of days, won't I?'

Andreas was privately amazed at her naivety. Surely she knew enough about the legal system to realise these things were not always clear-cut. But then, he reminded himself, she wanted that money and had gone to rather desperate means to access it. She hadn't factored in any last-minute hiccups once the marriage her father had insisted on had been achieved.

'It is very unlikely,' he informed her. 'I sought legal advice this morning. It could take months if not years to gain full access to your father's estate.'

Gemma's fork clattered against her plate as it fell from her fingers. '*Months?* But I have to have it now! I need it this week, or at least before we leave for Italy!'

'I can pay off your debts in the meantime,' he offered. 'Just tell me the amount and I will arrange for the amount to be deposited in your bank account.'

Gemma lowered her eyes to the food on her plate, her appetite completely disappearing. How could she tell him she needed a hundred thousand dollars, possibly more? Sure he was a billionaire, but it was still a huge amount of money. She considered telling him the truth, but wondered if he would believe her. Besides, she had to keep Rachel and Isabella safe for as long as she could. If the press got wind of this their lives could be in danger. She'd have to wait until Rachel and her daughter were safely in the States before she told him why she needed that money.

'It's very generous of you,' she mumbled.

'I am a rich man, Gemma. I am sure you have not accumulated enough bills to ruin me.'

She gave him a weak smile. 'Don't bet on it.'

'How much do you need?'

She took a steadying breath. 'A hundred thousand dollars...to start with...'

His brows rose slightly but he answered in an even tone. 'I will see that you have the money tomorrow.'

She compressed her lips to control the flood of relief that threatened to consume her.

'You *are* being honest with me, aren't you, Gemma?' he asked with a probing look cast her way. 'What we are talking about here are simple debts, not an out-of-control gambling or drug habit?'

She forced herself to meet his eyes, but her stomach felt as if a nest of large prickling ants had just been stirred up inside it. 'I am being honest with you. I have some debts, more than I'd like, but they have absolutely nothing to do with any vices other than an addiction to shopping.'

'Then I must say there is little evidence of your addiction,' he remarked wryly as his eyes ran over her simple, shapeless casual wear.

'I've got it under control now.'

'I have two sisters who will no doubt undo

your rehabilitation in one shopping expedition,' he said with a little smile that indicated his great fondness for his family.

'I will try and restrain myself.'

'You have no need to do so. I am, as I said earlier, a rich man. I can afford to dress you in whatever designer clothes you like. In fact I would prefer it if you would dress a little more extravagantly.'

'I don't like drawing attention to myself.'

'You have to let the past go, Gemma. You are a beautiful woman who should not be hiding behind a nun's habit or thereabouts.'

'Does your mistress dress flamboyantly?'

His mouth tightened. 'My relationship with Estella Garrison ended several months ago. We have remained business associates. I have just purchased a property on the central coast from her. She had no right to inform you of my dealings with Michael. I cannot think how she came by the knowledge. She may have over-heard a conversation or something. But believe me you have no need to be threatened by her.'

'I'm not the least bit threatened. You can have your dalliances, see if I care.'

'But you do care, *mia piccola*,' he said softly. 'I can see the hurt in your dark blue eyes even though you try so hard not to show it.'

'I'm not really in love with you,' she said, keeping her head well down. 'I was just pathetically grateful that you were able to unlock my…er…frigidity, that's all.'

'Glad to be of service.' He picked up his wineglass and took a leisurely sip before adding, 'But do not forget our agreement.'

'I haven't forgotten.'

'I want a child. We may well have conceived one already.'

Gemma felt the crush of her guilt press against her chest but she refused to meet his eyes in case he picked up on it. 'What is it about the arrogance of men who think that one sexual encounter will do the trick?'

'I am not intending there to be only one encounter,' he said in a low, sexy drawl that made the hairs on the back of her neck lift in awareness. 'I am planning on many encounters, all of them passionately fulfilling. You will be pregnant before the six months is up, I am sure. In fact I would hazard a guess that it will not even take that long.'

It will take for ever and a miracle besides, Gemma thought with a sinking feeling in the pit of her stomach.

'Come now, Gemma, eat up,' he said. 'This is a wonderful meal. You have done well. Where did you learn to cook like this? I had no idea you were so talented.'

Gemma picked up her cutlery even though she knew she wouldn't be able to eat much more than a mouthful. 'I did a course a couple of years ago. It was run by a chef who taught the basics. I've worked on from there. I enjoy it…fiddling with ingredients. After a lifetime of having food prepared for you in a hotel it's kind of nice to taste something home-cooked.'

'I applaud you for taking the time and trouble to do so,' he said. 'I am afraid I have been rather spoilt. I can manage a boiled egg but little else.'

'I can teach you, if you like.'

He smiled at her. 'Only if you let me teach you my language.'

She gave him a tremulous movement of her lips. 'It could take a long time, don't say I didn't warn you.'

He gave her another one of his long, thoughtful looks, but didn't respond. Gemma buried her head and began to eat almost mechanically in order to escape that penetrating gaze that continued to disturb her so much.

She knew she was being a fool for accepting his explanation about the woman who had called, and an even bigger fool for not taking him further to task over his bribery of Michael. Why had he done it? Was it just to get his hands on the hotel or was this his carefully orchestrated plan for revenge, to have her fall in love with him and then walk away as she had done to him?

CHAPTER FOURTEEN

ONCE their meal was cleared away Gemma made a move towards her room, but Andreas stalled her with a hand on her arm.

'We do not sleep alone in this marriage, *cara*. Not any longer.'

She looked down at his tanned hand on the creamy skin of her arm and suppressed a tiny shiver. 'Jealousy issues aside, I'm not the sharing type.'

He forced up her chin with his other hand, making her eyes mesh with his. 'I will say it again. I am not being unfaithful. I have wanted you for ten years and I still want you. There is no one else and will not be unless one or both of us calls an end to this marriage.'

Gemma wanted to trust him; everything in her insisted she put her pride aside and take what was on offer from him. After all, he had come to her rescue, even though he had coerced Michael to do it, marrying her, doing his best to secure her inheritance, even going so far as to step into the breach with this last distressing hiccup in proceedings.

Yes, she wasn't entirely sure of his motives for doing so, but so far he had not been unkind to her in any way, and if he said he wasn't involved with anyone else she should at least give him the benefit of the doubt, as indeed he had given her over her memory loss.

'I know you want me too,' Andreas said. 'There is no point trying to hide behind that wall of coldness you have erected around yourself for so long. I broke through it the other night and found a passionate young woman with needs and feelings that should not be denied any longer.'

'I didn't realise until the other night how terribly lonely I've been,' she confessed, surprising herself at her sudden candidness.

He pulled her up close, burying his head into the fragrant cloud of her hair. 'You have no need to be lonely now. We are in this together.'

But for how long? she wondered as his mouth

settled on hers, but within seconds she was lost to the heady sensation he was evoking within her. His tongue curled around hers, drawing a response from her that she had no hope of controlling. Within the space of minutes she was breathless and begging for the release his body promised in its heated trajectory as it pulsed against her.

There was no time for travelling to the bedroom; the huge leather sofa in the lounge was all the comfort they needed to revel in each other's bodies in a primitive coupling that was both urgent and tender at the same time.

Gemma sobbed her release, their breaths mingling with an intimacy she had not thought she would ever experience.

Within minutes he began stroking the slim length of her thighs and she was awakened again for his possession, her body craving his so much she reached for him with a boldness she had no idea she contained, her fingers stroking his length, marvelling at the way his body responded.

Shaking off her shyness, she shimmied down his body and caressed him with her mouth and tongue, relishing in the power she had over him, demonstrated by his deep, guttural groans.

'No…' he said, grasping her head in his hands. 'I cannot control myself.'

'Let me pleasure you.'

'Everything you do pleasures me. You do not have to…*Dio Mio.*'

Gemma rejoiced in the pulse of his body under her command, the intense intimacy of the contact beyond anything she had ever experienced.

'You are a goddess,' he said, pulling her back up to his chest after it was over. 'A bewitching goddess who is totally unforgettable.'

Gemma nestled up against him, her head on his chest where his heart was still thumping unevenly. 'I like the sound of that…' She sighed as her eyelashes closed over her eyes, the deep softness of the leather beneath her and the desire for sleep gradually drawing her away from her conscious attempt to separate the truth from her lies. 'You are totally unforgettable too.'

The flight to Naples was to Gemma unlike the last time she had travelled overseas. Although

246 BEDDED AND WEDDED FOR REVENGE

she had flown first class when she had flown
with her father and stepmother when she was a
teenager, the private jet Andreas had waiting for
him at the airport surpassed anything she had
ever dreamed of.

They were swiftly waved through Customs
and met at the gate by one of the Trigliani staff
members who doubled as a chauffeur.

He greeted Gemma with a type of warmth
she found reassuring, hoping the reception
Andreas's family gave her was equally friendly.

The picturesque villa Andreas owned was in
the little village of L'Annunziata, perched on a
summit of a hill overlooking the Island of Capri
and the Gulf of Naples. The village was situated
ten kilometres from Sorrento, giving you access
to both Naples and Capri, and eighteen kilometres from Positano, Andreas informed her
proudly on the journey.

Gemma couldn't hold back her pleasure at
seeing Andreas's family holiday residence. The
gardens positively spilled over their beds with
glorious colourful blooms and the air was scented
with the sea far below as well as the sweet, heady
lemon blossoms from the surrounding hills.

'It's so…beautiful…' she breathed in wonder, taking the hand he offered her as he guided her up the steps leading to the front entrance. 'It's the most wonderful place I've ever seen.'

Andreas smiled down at her and led her forward to where his mother and two heavily pregnant sisters were waiting with open arms and a rush of staccato Italian that left her ears ringing.

She was enveloped in a crushing hug by each woman in turn, and then kissed on both cheeks by Andreas's two brothers-in-law who patiently waited their turn.

'My mother speaks a little English, but I will interpret for you if things prove too difficult for you or her,' Andreas explained. 'Lucia and Gianna and Paolo and Ricardo are fluent, or at least as much as me.'

The barrier of language didn't appear to be a problem as Gemma was treated like a princess from the moment she stepped inside the ancient villa.

The next few days passed in a blur of sunshine, good food and gentle exercise in the pool situated at the back of the villa where the sun drenched the garden in heady, healing rays.

Andreas seemed intent on showing her every-thing, the towns of Sorrento and Positano were explored in detail, exquisite food eaten at the restaurants and cafés, and his sisters promised that if they were not so close to delivering their babies they would have whipped her away to Rome or Milan for a shopping trip to make her holiday all the more perfect.

'I'm not really much of a shopper,' Gemma had laughingly replied, feeling relaxed and happy in a way she hadn't in years, perhaps had never felt, until she glanced at Andreas and saw his frown, and the questioning look that crossed his face.

Andreas had been as good as his word and deposited the funds she'd requested in her bank account, and within minutes she had used her telephone banking service to transfer the full amount to Rachel's account. She'd also organised the flights so all Rachel had to do was pick up the tickets from the local travel agent. The comfort she drew from knowing Rachel and Isabella were now well on their way to the States to receive the help Isabella needed had placed Gemma in a state close to euphoria. So too had the tender and sensuous attention Andreas bathed her in, leaving her senses in an almost constant state of physical alert when he was anywhere nearby.

She refused to think about the court case waiting for when they returned to Sydney. She knew the fight with Marcia would be dirty and long, but Gemma's immediate problems had been solved, or at least would be once Isabella was given the all clear. Then and only then would she feel safe enough to tell Andreas how she had spent his money. Once her father's estate was secured she would pay it back in full. That was her only comfort in the deception she'd had to continue for this long.

'What was this I heard about huge credit-card bills?' Lucia teased as she reached for her tall glass of fresh orange juice. 'My brother said you are…what is it in English…a connoisseur of consumerism?'

'That is correct,' Andreas said with an unreadable look as he captured Gemma's eyes. 'Gemma has but one vice. She has a compulsion to shop.'

'Then you are in very good company,' Paolo said earning a playful dig in the ribs from his wife.

The lively exchange continued but without

Gemma's input. She felt the tension building behind her eyes, distorting her vision and making nausea rise in her throat.

'Are you all right?' Gianna asked after a few minutes.

Gemma gave her a weak smile. 'I'm not feeling well. I think I've had too much sun.'

'Perhaps you are pregnant,' Lucia suggested. 'I was sick almost from the first moment.'

'No,' Gemma said without thinking. 'I couldn't possibly be pregnant. It's just a headache. I'll lie down for a while and I'll be fine.'

Andreas's mother shooed him away once one of the girls had translated the situation and ushered her new daughter-in-law into the cool interior of the villa and helped her into bed, fussing over her just as a real mother would have done.

Gemma had a hard time containing her emotion at the gentle loving care she was being given, hating herself for the deceit that had led to a situation that was fast getting out of control.

She had seen suspicion in Andreas's dark eyes when she'd made that little slip about shopping. How else would she have supposedly run up numerous bills?

Her stomach heaved in alarm. What she had always suspected was true.

He didn't believe her.

But why hadn't he confronted her with it?

What was he waiting for?

She had already told him she was in love with him, several times. She hadn't been able to help herself. Meeting his family had made her fall in love with him all over again. She felt she knew him even more now that she was surrounded by those who loved and knew him best.

But he hadn't said a thing about his own feelings. He had shown her passion and desire—yes, and he'd been exquisitely tender out of consideration for her painful past, although true to his promise he had not referred to that night again.

She couldn't make him out. She was almost certain he had revenge on his mind but so far she saw no sign of it.

For some reason the lurking threat of it was all the more intimidating…

Gemma heard him enter their room later that evening, carrying a tray of food prepared by the family housekeeper.

'My mother thought you might be hungry,' he said, closing the door behind him with his foot.

'I'm not.'

'You should eat,' he insisted. 'If you are indeed carrying my child as Lucia suggested you must eat even when you don't feel like it.'

'I'm not pregnant.'

His eyes were very focused on hers. 'You seem very sure of that.'

'I know my own body.'

'When is your monthly period due?'

She rolled her eyes. 'Oh, *please*, do we have to have this discussion now?'

'Yes, I think we do.' He put the tray down on the bedside table and sat on the edge of the bed near her stiff legs.

'I told you I'm not ready to have a child.'

'Are you doing anything actively to avoid it?' he asked.

'You can inspect my toiletries for pills and diaphragms, but, no—I'm not doing anything actively to avoid it.'

'It is not simply a mind-over-matter issue, Gemma. Unprotected sex normally leads to pregnancy in the matter of a few months if the sex is frequent enough.'

'I'm not in the mood if that is why you're here.'

He ran a hand through his hair. 'If you think I am the sort of man who would insist on my conjugal rights when you are unwell then your opinion of me is something I will have to work on a little more assiduously.'

'I'd like to be left alone,' she said, turning her back.

There was a creeping silence. Gemma felt it coming towards her inexorably, like a curl of acrid smoke actively seeking her next indrawn breath so it could poison her lungs.

'What did you do with the money I gave you?' Andreas asked.

Gemma's fingers on the sheet tightened. 'I spent it.'

'On what?'

'Bills.'

'I have your credit-card statements in my briefcase downstairs. You haven't used a credit card for something like two years.'

Gemma knew she was trapped. She hunted

her brain for a reasonable excuse for why she had dispensed with such a large amount of cash but her post-migraine head refused to co-operate. She tried to reassure herself that he couldn't possibly have seen the flights she'd booked on her credit card as the statement wouldn't be due until the following month, but how could she be sure? He seemed to have an uncanny ability to find things out about her affairs.

'I will ask you again, Gemma. Do you have a drug or gambling problem?'

'No.'

'Is someone blackmailing you?'

God, she thought, mentally kicking herself. *Why hadn't she thought of that?*

'Gemma?' he prompted.

'No…I…I leant it to a friend.'

'Who?'

'I can't say.'

'Why not?'

'Because…'

'Because why?'

'Because my friend needs me not to tell anyone.' She flipped over to her back so she could meet his eyes. 'I can't tell you any more than that. I'm afraid you'll just have to trust me.'

'Is this friend going to pay you back?'

She lowered her eyes from the sudden intensity of his and whispered, 'No.'

'I see.' His voice was tight. 'So you gave away a hundred thousand dollars of my money that you are at this point not even sure you are going to get from your father's estate to pay me back, to someone whom you will not reveal the identity of, and I am supposed to be content with that explanation?'

'I *will* pay you back,' she said. 'I swear to God I will pay you back if it takes me a lifetime to do it.'

'It should only take you nine months to do it,' he said, getting to his feet, his expression white-tipped with anger.

'I'm not a breeding machine,' she tossed at him furiously.

He turned from the door and gave her a cutting look. 'And I am not a money machine.'

The door clicked on his exit, the sharp sound feeling like a slap to Gemma's still tender head.

She sank back amongst the pillows and fought against the despair that threatened to consume her, but it was hopeless. The stoicism that had been her trademark for so long was too far out of reach. Tears ran in streams down her cheeks, her only consolation that no sound accompanied their crystal progress…

CHAPTER FIFTEEN

ALTHOUGH she was certain no one in Andreas's family would have picked up on it, Gemma was conscious of his brooding anger and distance whenever they were alone. He put on a good show when family members were about, sitting on the arm of her chair, tending her needs just as devotedly as his brothers-in-law did to his sisters, but at night he slept well away from her in the big bed, not once reaching for her as he had done so many times before.

She lay awake for hours, aching to close the distance in the bed, but her pride felt too bruised. If he had told her he loved her she would have thrown herself at him, perhaps even trusted him enough to tell him the truth about Isabella, but without that declaration she couldn't risk he might seek the revenge he clearly wanted in the most devastating way of all. She tried to tell herself he would never act so despicably, but how could she be sure? Isabella's own father had injured her for no reason at all. Andreas on the other hand had many reasons for wanting to inflict hurt on Gemma for what she had done to him. He had already bribed Michael out of marrying her; what other lengths would he go to in order to achieve his ends?

Two days before they were scheduled to leave, Lucia announced her baby was on the way, and within hours of her being admitted to hospital Gianna clutched at her belly and made the very same announcement.

The villa was in an excited uproar and Gemma was swept up in it, even though there was immense pain in it for her as she knew that what both Lucia and Gianna were experiencing was never going to happen to her.

Lucia gave birth to a baby boy at four that afternoon and Gianna delivered a little girl three hours later. The babies were beautiful and brought much needed joy to Andreas's mother who had waited so long for grandchildren to fil the aching emptiness of her loss.

Paolo handed his baby son to Gemma to hold and she took the infant with hands not quite steady, unable to control the emotion clogging her chest. She gazed down in wonder at the tiny perfection of the infant in her arms, the little starfish hands, the minuscule perfection of his fingernails and his little rosebud mouth that seemed to be already searching for sustenance. She couldn't speak even though she wanted to say how thrilled she was for them all, but the words couldn't get past the aching lump lodged in her throat. Tears burned in her eyes and her chest felt heavy and aching with regret.

She was relieved when they were all ushered out of the hospital to allow the new mothers some rest.

Andreas was quiet on the drive back to the villa. He barely looked in her direction, his expression closed.

'It was nice that you got to meet your niece and nephew before we leave,' she offered into the silence.

'Yes.'

'Andreas…' She moistened her mouth and tried again. 'I really like your family. You are very lucky.'

He flicked a quick glance her way, but didn't respond.

Gemma sat back in her seat and sighed. It was going to be a long trip home.

The flight back to Australia was exhausting for Gemma notwithstanding the luxury treatment the staff on Andreas's private jet lavished on her.

She was relieved when they finally made it back to his house where Susanne had already turned back the bed for her.

'I thought you might be a little jet-lagged,' the housekeeper said. 'Andreas seems to cope with it pretty well, but you don't strike me as the resilient sort.'

Gemma gave her a wan smile. 'I feel like the jet I've just been flying in has backed over me several times with the luggage still on board.'

Susanne gave her a comforting pat as she pulled the sheet over her. 'It will pass. Close your eyes and get some sleep. I'll leave a nice dinner for you when you wake up. Andreas has gone to the office; he should be back in an hour or so.'

'Thank you, Susanne. You're being so kind to me. I really appreciate it.'

'It's no trouble,' she said. 'What did you think of the Trigliani family?'

'They were wonderful,' she said. 'I wish I'd had such a family when I was young. No wonder Andreas is so…so…'

'So lovable?'

Gemma felt her chest tighten. 'Yes…but he doesn't love me.'

'What was that we were saying about words and actions the other day?' Susanne reminded her as she gave the bed a final pat. 'Don't go paying any attention to words unless the actions back them up.'

Gemma settled amongst the soft linen as Susanne left the room and thought about the housekeeper's comment. Andreas hadn't spoken of his feelings, but at times his actions hinted at very deep feelings, feelings perhaps he was not yet willing to articulate.

Could it be he had never fallen out of love with her, in spite of how she had treated him? That he was holding her at a distance now because he needed more time to learn to trust her? She had hurt him in the cruellest way; it would take a lot of courage to make himself so vulnerable again.

Gemma drifted in and out of a hazy sleep, the sunlight coming into the room making it hard for her to totally relax, and then, just as she thought she was going to finally drift off, she heard the doorbell ring downstairs.

She waited for Susanne to answer it, but, glancing at the clock by the bedside, realised the housekeeper would have left for the day at least an hour ago.

She considered ignoring the consistent peeling of the door bell, but it seemed someone was very determined to be acknowledged, so, rustling herself into a bathrobe, she made her way down the stairs to the front door.

'Michael!' She stared down at him in surprise. 'I thought you were overseas.'

'I'm leaving next week,' he said, then, looking up at his partner standing next to his chair, asked him to wait in the van and that he would only be a few minutes.

Gemma watched as the other man walked back to the van parked outside before she opened the door wider so Michael could activate his chair to come in.

'How are you, Gemma?' Michael asked once they were in the lounge.

'I'm fine. How are you?' She gave him a hard little look. 'Enjoying your newfound financial independence provided by my husband?'

He gave her a tortured glance before staring down at his hands. 'I knew you would be angry with me but I thought it was the best thing. If it's any comfort to you I only took the money because Andreas insisted.'

'How very considerate of you.'

Michael looked uncomfortable, his gaze going anywhere but near hers. 'I had a visit from your stepmother,' he said after a lengthy pause.

'Oh?' Gemma sat on the edge of the sofa so he didn't have to crane his neck in case by some sort of miracle he decided to meet her eyes. 'What did she want?'

'She told me she's contesting your father's will.'

'Yes…I had heard that.'

He brought his eyes to hers. 'Gemma…' he cleared his throat and continued '…there are things about…that night that I remember.'

Gemma sat up straighter, her body suddenly

tense and on high alert. 'You've got your memory back?'

He looked away again and stared at the Persian rug on the floor, his voice a low mumble as he confessed, 'I didn't lose it in the first place.'

She stared at him speechlessly, shock filling her like ice in her veins. Her chest tightened with such pain she could hardly breathe. Why had he lied to her for all this time?

She took a convulsive swallow. *'You what?'*

'When I woke up from the medically induced coma I was dazed for a long time. My father told me you had been charged with negligent driving and that I was certain to get a huge insurance payout as a result. He also told me you were suffering from amnesia. You didn't remember a thing about the accident or what had occurred before it.'

Gemma felt as if something cold, hard and sharp was forcing its way down her spine, keeping her rigid in her seat. She couldn't speak. The words she most wanted to ask were locked somewhere between her throat and her aching chest.

'He told me that I wouldn't be paid a cent if it came out that I was the driver,' Michael added.

'But you weren't the driver,' Gemma said, her brain feeling like wet cotton wool as she tried to make sense of what he was saying. 'It was my car. I had come to your house that night. You told me that yourself. I was upset, you said, and you suggested we go for a drive as your father had guests at your place.'

Michael met her confused gaze. 'Yes, you were upset. You'd had a monumental argument with Marcia. I was worried about you. You were hysterical, so I suggested I drive instead. We switched seats but before we could put on our seat belts a dog came out of nowhere and I swerved to miss it and hit the tree instead.'

'I wasn't driving...' Gemma couldn't stop saying the words, even though they were only coming out as a faint, hoarse whisper. 'I wasn't driving...*I wasn't driving...*'

'No, Gemma,' he said heavily. 'The accident was my fault. I shouldn't have started driving until we were both in our seat belts but I didn't stop to think. I just wanted to take you away someplace safe so you could tell me what had happened between your stepmother and you.'

Gemma finally managed to stop mechanically

chanting long enough to think to ask, 'And did I tell you what the argument was about?'

He shook his head. 'No, you were crying so hard I couldn't get it out of you. I'm sorry, I wish I could tell you but the only person who can tell you what happened that night if you don't remember it yourself is your stepmother.'

Gemma felt her whole body slump in defeat. She pinched the bridge of her nose, forcing herself to think, wishing she could squeeze the memory out of the recesses of her brain, but it was all a blank.

A hopeless, useless blank.

'I'm sorry, Gemma,' Michael said into the painful silence. 'I should have confessed the truth a long time ago, but I needed that money. I know you will find it hard to forgive, but I figured you came from a wealthy background. I had nothing. The insurance payout has set me up. I can live more or less independently now.'

'You betrayed me…' Gemma found it hard to even say the words, unwilling to admit them out loud. The one person she had trusted over all others had in the end betrayed her.

'I didn't intend to,' he said, his voice cracking

slightly over the words. 'Things just got complicated. I thought it was the best way out. You
didn't remember the accident or what led up to
it, the doctors said it was unlikely you ever
would. I kind of figured my secret would be
safe. Your father paid your bail. There was no
other choice for me.'

'What changed your mind?'

'I felt guilty about Andreas buying me off. I
would have left it alone, but, as I told you, your
stepmother came to see me,' he said. 'There was
something about her that I hadn't seen before, a
chilling sort of ruthlessness. She will stop at
nothing to get what she wants. I hadn't seen that
in her before, in spite of the things you often said
she did and said to you.'

'What did she say to you?'

'She tried to blackmail me,' he said. 'I think
your father must have guessed the truth about
the accident. That's probably why he con-
tacted Andreas Trigliani as he presumed I
would be an obvious choice of husband to
fulfil his terms.'

'Whose own bribe you readily accepted?'
Gemma said, her tone laced with accusation.

His eyes moved away from hers again. 'I would rather accept money from a man like Andreas Trigliani than be toyed with by someone like your stepmother.'

Gemma couldn't help agreeing with him even though it pained her to admit it.

'I hated lying to you, Gemma,' he said. 'You have been the one friend who has stood by me all these years. What I have done to you is unforgivable. I wish I could rewrite the past but no one can. We've both in our different ways paid a huge price for stupid mistakes. I only hope you can find some happiness now as I have found with Jeremy waiting for me outside.'

'Thank you for telling me,' Gemma finally managed to say, but it was all she could get past her burning, tight throat.

'Goodbye, Gemma. I probably won't see you again. I think it's best.'

Gemma couldn't speak as she assisted him to the door. She stood in its frame and watched as Jeremy came up and helped Michael into the van with loving concern.

She closed the door and leaned against it once they had driven off, her mind spinning off in all

directions with such force she didn't at first recognise she wasn't alone.

She looked up and saw Susanne standing there
with a duster in her hand, her face a picture of in-
credulity, not unlike what Gemma was still feeling.

'I didn't leave at my usual time,' the housekeeper explained. 'I didn't hear the doorbell at
first; I was putting rubbish out. I thought I'd stay
a bit longer as I was worried about you. Are you
all right?'

Gemma pushed herself away from the door.
'I think so.'

'I heard most of it,' Susanne confessed. 'I think
you should tell Andreas immediately.'

Gemma turned to look at her. 'He won't
believe me.'

'Then I will tell him.'

'You can if you like, but there's something I
have to do first,' Gemma said as she reached
for the phone.

'What are you doing?' Susanne asked.

'I'm calling for a taxi,' Gemma answered. 'I
think it's time my stepmother and I had a little
chat.'

Susanne pushed the phone out of her hand.

'You don't need to call a taxi. I'll take you myself.'

Gemma released the phone. 'I don't want to embroil you in something like this.'

Susanne gave her a smile. 'We're friends, right? Friends stand beside each other. You need backup right now and, since your husband is un-available, I will have to step in.'

'I can't ask you do to this.'

'You're not asking me.' Susanne grabbed her bag and keys and hastily scribbled a note and left it on the hall table. 'Come on. We're on a hunt for the truth and, let me tell you, I'm like Sherlock Holmes when it comes to the truth. I don't stop until I uncover it.'

Gemma followed in her wake, wondering what Andreas was going to say when he came home and found both his housekeeper and wife gone without trace.

CHAPTER SIXTEEN

MARCIA LANDERSTALLE had clearly not been expecting visitors and at first refused to answer the door of her penthouse suite at The Landerstalle Hotel.

Susanne pulled some strings with one of the managers and brandished a skeleton key as she rejoined Gemma. 'It always pays to have connections,' she said with a little smile of victory.

'You're really good at this,' Gemma remarked. 'I'm quaking in my shoes, but you're taking this all in your stride.'

'Yes, well, I've had to deal with difficult people all my life,' Susanne said and she rapped at the door again. 'Come on, Marcia. I've got a key. Either you let us in or we come in. Your choice.'

The door opened after a slight pause and Gemma came face to face with her stepmother for the first time in nearly five and a half years.

Marcia's cold light blue gaze stripped Gemma. 'You've put on weight, I see. I told you you would if you didn't control yourself.'

Gemma fought against the emotional backlash the cruel taunt evoked, trying not to recall the many times she had engaged in self-abuse to rid her mind of those vicious jibes.

'Come on, Marcia,' Susanne sprang to Gemma's defence. 'Didn't you know that middle age spread wasn't something you ate but something you were supposed to avoid?'

Gemma felt the urge to giggle at Susanne's acerbic wit, but the seriousness of the situation called for solemnity.

She faced her stepmother squarely, calling on the acting skill she had been putting in practice with Andreas. 'I thought I should inform you that I finally remember what happened the night of my accident. My amnesia is no longer. I have remembered everything.'

As ploys went it certainly worked if the pallor of Marcia's face was anything to go by. Gemma watched as the older woman sank to the nearest sofa, her hands visibly shaking.

But before Gemma could say anything else

there was a sound behind her and she turned to see Andreas framed in the doorway.

Susanne ushered him in, murmuring something to him in an undertone.

Gemma met his gaze briefly, surprised to find his eyes warm as they connected with hers.

She reluctantly turned back to face her stepmother. 'Why don't you save me the trouble of recounting that night and tell it in your own words?' she suggested, taking a risk she wasn't sure was going to pay off.

Marcia's eyes flickered to Andreas, then to Susanne and back to Gemma. 'I don't know what you're talking about.'

'I think you do,' Gemma said. 'Michael Carter came to see me this evening. He told me the truth about what I told him the night I went to his house, how upset I was after yet another run-in with you.'

'You're lying,' Marcia said. 'You don't remember a thing.'

'I remember a lot more than you realise,' Gemma said.

'You're trying to threaten me to scare me off fighting for your father's estate,' Marcia said.

'He would have left you with everything without question if he didn't have doubts,' Gemma pointed out.

'You've always been a lying little cow,' Marcia snarled. 'Look at the way you treated Andreas here. The whole staff was talking about it for weeks afterwards. You lied to gain favour with your father. Andreas hadn't done a thing to you, but you wilfully ruined his reputation by asserting he had. You're a cold-hearted little bitch who didn't even have the grace to make peace with your father before he died.'

'You have the choice to tell it your way or hear my version,' Gemma challenged. 'Somehow the courts might not take too kindly to hearing the truth about what happened that night.'

'She is right.' Andreas stepped forward, placing a gentle and protective arm around Gemma's waist. 'It is time for you to tell the truth or have it told for you. I have engaged a legal team who assure me they will make mincemeat of your claims to Lionel Landerstalle's estate. You have not got a hope, not unless you are willing to put everything you own on the line. The court case could go on for years. I have enough money to fuel it indefinitely but you do not.'

The defeat flickered on Marcia's face but it was clear she wasn't going down without a last-minute fight. 'I'm glad I did what I did,' she snarled viciously. 'You deserved it, you little bitch, for being so difficult. I tried my best with you over the years but you refused to accept me. I wanted a child but your father wouldn't hear of it. He was fed up with how difficult you were and refused to take a chance on having another child in case he or she turned out spoilt and wilful like you. You ruined my life and I thought it was high time you were taught a lesson.'

Gemma felt her throat move up and down as her stepmother's gaze burned into hers. 'You were being your usual flirtatious self at your party,' Marcia continued. 'But for once you weren't drinking. One of the guests who had come with one of your so-called girlfriends had his eye on you all evening and I told him you liked him. I suggested he take you a drink and take things from there.'

Gemma felt the tightening of Andreas's arm around her as the memory of that evening returned with brutal force. She clamped her eyes shut, but it only made it worse. The only thing that held her together was the strong fortress of Andreas beside her.

'I didn't know he would lace your drink with a party drug,' Marcia said, although she showed no regret on her face or in her tone.

'That's what the argument the night of the accident was about, wasn't it?' Andreas asked the question Gemma would have asked if she could have located her voice. 'You told Gemma what you had done by encouraging that low-life creep to abuse her in such a despicable way. You told her how you had vicariously destroyed her life in a petty payback that had devastating consequences for her.'

Marcia put up her chin. 'She asked for it. She was always prancing about as if she was better than anyone else. Besides, I thought there was a rough sort of justice in it. After all, she had cried wolf over your treatment of her. I thought it was only fair that no one believed her when the tables were turned.'

'So you took it into your own hands and ruined her young life as if it meant nothing?' he accused, the red hot anger running through his voice unmistakable.

'She deserved it,' Marcia bit out. 'You of all people should agree with me. Isn't that why you married her—to get revenge for what she did to you?'

Gemma felt her breath come to a screeching halt in her chest. She couldn't look at Andreas in case she saw the truth of her stepmother's words reflected in the dark gaze she had come to love so much.

'I do not wish to discuss my reasons for marrying Gemma with someone like you,' he said. 'All I will say is I am glad I did so. I have not regretted a single day of my marriage.'

Gemma heard someone sobbing and realised it was Susanne, her face buried in a handkerchief.

'Lionel Landerstalle trusted me enough to take care of his daughter and I took his trust very seriously,' Andreas went on. 'I suggest you cancel your lawyer. You have no hope of winning this case. Gemma may have some lapses in her memory, but I have done some investigations of my own and the one thing her father knew was

278 BEDDED AND WEDDED FOR REVENGE

that you were having an affair a few months
before he died. The on-and-off-again affair that
Gemma had discovered you were having just
before her accident, which, conveniently for you,
she had lost the memory of relaying to you.'

'She should have died in that accident,' Marcia
said with a venomous glare. 'She ruined my life
with Lionel. She came between us constantly
from the word go. I only had the affair because
I was so unhappy because of her.'

'She was just a child,' Andreas said. 'You were
the adult. It was up to you to make the necessary
adjustments—'

'No, wait,' Gemma interrupted, turning from
the shelter of Andreas's arms to face her stepmother. 'Marcia…I have many regrets about
how I behaved when you first came on the scene.
Andreas is to some degree right in that I was just
a child, but I was a very spoilt child and I didn't
really give you a chance. I made your life hell.
I was jealous and missed my mother. I know
you are not essentially a bad person; I'm not
sure anyone really is deep inside.' She took a
shaky breath and continued, 'I am so deeply
ashamed that you weren't able to have the child

you desperately wanted. I didn't realise I had caused my father to deny you that right.'

'*Cara,*' Andreas began with a cautionary hand on her arm, but she ignored him and went on regardless. 'Please, Marcia. Forgive me for what I did. You didn't deserve to be treated like that and I'm sorry.'

Marcia's face crumpled and she shook her head in remorse and regret for what she had done. Before Andreas could stop her, Gemma had broken free from his protective hold to embrace her stepmother.

It was some minutes before Marcia and Gemma separated; both of their faces were ravaged by tears, but Andreas had never felt such pride in all his life at the way Gemma gently spoke to her stepmother as they were finally leaving.

'You can have whatever you want from my father's estate,' she said. 'I just need enough funds to see me through for the next couple of months. I also need to pay Andreas back, but the rest is yours. I would have liked to give you the hotel but I promised Andreas I would sell it to him, but perhaps we can come to some arrangement—you know, where you live in the hotel rent-free.'

Marcia nodded, unable to speak.

'Come, *piccola*,' Andreas said wryly. 'My housekeeper is—what do you call it in English? Turning into a basket case?'

Gemma smiled at Susanne, who was still doing her best to mop up her tears. 'She's not a basket case, Andreas. She's a woman with a soft heart.'

'*Dio Mio!*' He slapped his head theatrically with his hand. 'Do not tell me I have now two such women in my life.'

It was immensely frustrating to Gemma to have to wait until Susanne had been escorted to her car before she could speak privately with Andreas.

She considered doing so in the car on the way back to his house, but decided to wait until they were both inside without the distraction of driving through traffic.

Andreas took her into his arms as soon as they entered the house, but, although Gemma longed for the comfort of his arms, she knew she had things to confess.

'Andreas…I need to talk to you.'

'I am tired of talking,' he said. 'I want to make love to you.'

She peered up into his eyes. 'Did you really mean it when you said you were glad you married me and that you hadn't regretted a single day?'

He gave her a rueful smile. 'I was not ready to admit it until this evening, but, yes, I am very glad I married you. I admit I had nefarious motives for doing so. I had devised various plans for revenge, but seeing you again changed all that. You had changed. As much as I fought it I fell in love with you all over again, but even more hopelessly this time.'

'I have a confession to make,' she said, unable to meet his eyes. 'I have memory loss, great holes of it which frustrate me daily, but the one thing I have never forgotten is how I treated you.' She raised her eyes back to his. 'Can you ever forgive me for that, both for treating you that way and also for lying to you so often in the last few weeks?'

He smiled as he drew her closer. 'I had already begun to suspect you had not forgotten me, *cara*. I felt it in your kiss, the touch of your hands and the way your eyes avoided mine so often.'

'You knew?'

He smiled. 'You are not a very good liar, *cara*. Did I not tell you that before? You made many little slips and I was storing them up, ready to call you to account, when I realised I loved you too much to hurt you.'

'There's something else...' She lowered her gaze again.

'If you are about to confess about where the hundred thousand dollars went, I already know.'

She blinked at him in shock. *'You do?'*

'I had a paper trail done, but don't worry, no one else will find out. I realised it must be someone from the shelter you were helping. The private investigator I engaged told me it had to remain a secret for the mother and child's protection. He was concerned he might have frightened your friend. He had been following a little too closely and she had seemed very agitated. But they are perfectly safe now and you should hear soon if the operation has been a success.'

Gemma felt relief flood through her that he

finally knew but there was just one more secret she had to confess.

She took a deep, steadying breath. 'Um… there's something else I have to tell you.'

'Must we waste time with all these confessions when all I want to do is claim you as my own?' he asked. 'I want to make love to you. I am bursting with the need to do so.'

She lifted her troubled eyes to his. 'I can't give you what you want, Andreas. You said when you offered to marry me that I was to give you a child. It was part of the deal.'

'Do not worry, *mia piccola*, I know you need more time. We will not rush things. When the time is right it will happen.'

'But that's what I'm trying to tell you, Andreas,' she said, bordering on despair. 'I am unable to have children.'

He stared at her for a long time, his expression giving nothing away.

'It was the accident.' She filled the silence. 'The doctor said I would probably need IVF to conceive. It would take a miracle for it to happen any other way.'

Andreas held her close, his heart beating

solidly, firmly against hers. 'Then we will hope and pray for a miracle and if one does not occur then we will go looking for one by some other means, all right?'

She looked up at him and smiled, her heart feeling as if it were taking up all the available room in her chest. 'All right,' she said, her eyes shining with joy. 'I'll start praying right now.'

He pulled her even closer. 'You can do that later, but in the meantime I have something else in mind.'

'I'm not sure I'm game enough to ask what it is,' she said as he began to nuzzle her neck, her skin shivering all over. 'Is it something I'm going to enjoy?'

He lifted his head to give her a smoulderingly sexy look.

'You are not just going to enjoy it—you are never going to forget it for the rest of your life.'

And nine months later when their tiny son was born, Gemma had to agree that he was absolutely right.

MILLS & BOON® PUBLISH EIGHT LARGE PRINT TITLES A MONTH. THESE ARE THE EIGHT TITLES FOR JUNE 2007.

❦

TAKEN BY THE SHEIKH
Penny Jordan

THE GREEK'S VIRGIN
Trish Morey

THE FORCED BRIDE
Sara Craven

BEDDED AND WEDDED FOR REVENGE
Melanie Milburne

RANCHER AND PROTECTOR
Judy Christenberry

THE VALENTINE BRIDE
Liz Fielding

ONE SUMMER IN ITALY...
Lucy Gordon

CROWNED: AN ORDINARY GIRL
Natasha Oakley

MILLS & BOON®

MILLS & BOON PUBLISH EIGHT LARGE PRINT TITLES A MONTH. THESE ARE THE EIGHT TITLES FOR JULY 2007.

❧

ROYALLY BEDDED, REGALLY WEDDED
Julia James

THE SHEIKH'S ENGLISH BRIDE
Sharon Kendrick

SICILIAN HUSBAND, BLACKMAILED BRID
Kate Walker

AT THE GREEK BOSS'S BIDDING
Jane Porter

CATTLE RANCHER, CONVENIENT WIFE
Margaret Way

BAREFOOT BRIDE
Jessica Hart

THEIR VERY SPECIAL GIFT
Jackie Braun

HER PARENTHOOD ASSIGNMENT
Fiona Harper

MILLS & BOON®